Generation Dead

Book One. Becoming

Joseph Talluto

CHAPTER 1

"They're right outside the door."

"What?"

"They're right outside the door."

"I'm sorry, I can't hear you. What?"

"Jesus Christ, you're a pain in the ass. "

"That's not nice."

"Oh, so you *can* hear me, huh?"

"Shut up."

I shook my head as I chuckled softly to myself. It was the same old story with my older brother Jake. He never took the dead seriously, never felt like they were any real danger, and as a result, managed to put us into some serious situations time and time again.

"Where's Julia?" Jake asked.

"She's probably somewhere safe where she doesn't have to worry about the zombies that *you* managed to alert." We had been through this before, and I had never seen anyone with so little concern for their own safety when it came to becoming infected.

"Whatever," Jake said. "May as well get this over with." He walked over to the bedroom door and hefted his weapon. It was, for all intents and purposes, a mace. It had a twenty-inch handle, topped with a hunk of metal shaped into four pyramids. The pyramids were barely two inches high, but they were devastating on zombie skulls. The best part was they rarely broke open the skull. They just crushed it inward.

"Wait!" I whispered, but it was too late. Jake had already opened the door.

Before the door was even open, Jake was swinging his weapon, crushing the skull of the nearest zombie and cracking the head of another before the zombies even knew what was happening. Jake took a step back and let the two of them fall, making the rest of the zombies come to him through the narrow doorway. As the next ones tripped and fell, Jake killed them with silent efficiency. All I had to do was watch. My own weapon was out, but I had a feeling Jake wasn't going to need my help.

Suddenly, I heard a noise. At first, I wasn't sure what it was, but then I heard the distinct sound of someone yelling for help. That can't be Julia, I thought. She was way too good at what we do to get herself into any trouble. She certainly wouldn't be yelling, especially considering where we were.

I heard it again, and this time it was louder and much clearer. "Aaron! Help!" Yep, it was Julia, and yep, she was in trouble. Problem was, Jake was blocking my exit, cheerfully killing zombies as they kept trying to get at the meal that just wouldn't lie down quietly and be eaten.

I looked out the window, made some mental calculations, and cursed. "Fuck it." I opened the side bedroom window, and climbed out, bracing my feet on the windowsill of the building we were in and the one next door. Barely three feet separated the buildings in this part of Chicago, so it wasn't difficult to do. I braced my foot on a spot two feet higher, and then pushed hard, bringing my other foot up and to a higher place on the other building. I tried to ignore the zombies on the ground below me, which from my perspective, looked as if they were reaching up for my crotch. That sight will motivate you more than anything you could imagine.

I reached the next floor up and thankfully got my feet on the sills. I took a breath, and then looked in the window at the situation. There were six zombies in the bedroom, and they were gathered around what looked to be a closet. I had a feeling I knew where Julia was.

That was the good news. The bad news was that, since I was on the ledge right next to them, they couldn't help but see me. The ones closest to me almost seemed surprised that another idiot was so close, just for the taking. They came over to the window and began scratching and beating at it with dead, skeletal hands. Two of them pressed their dark grey faces to the window, smearing it with foul fluids and biting at it with rotton teeth.

Since I had to break the window anyway, I figured I might as well make it productive. I took out my hand axe, the one with a pointed spike opposite the axe head, and took careful aim. It wasn't easy to swing something with any degree of accuracy while being spread-eagled between two buildings, and forty feet in the air.

The spike crashed through the window and punched through the forehead of the zombie nearest me. Its eyes rolled up into its head and I jerked the spike free as it fell. I killed the next one that stuck its head out the window, and barely managed to get my leg out of the way of a shorter one that came reaching for a snack. I spiked his head, and then looked full in the face of a zombie that came charging through the window. I could do nothing to stop him, but I did watch him fall down between the buildings and land on another zombie with a wet, splattering sound.

I had both feet on the ledge of the opposite building, and held myself away from the broken window with my axe. Another zombie came charging out and fell the same way with a disappointed splat at the end. The next two followed suit, and there was a pile of arms, legs and writhing zombies underneath me that looked really disgusting. I couldn't help myself. "Get a room!" I called down to the zombies. I think one answered me.

I looked through the window and saw the coast was clear. I carefully climbed through, trying not to cut myself on the smeared glass. The room was identical to the one I had just left, except this one was decorated in a much more subdued style. The dresser was open, and clothing lay on the floor, signs of a hurried exit. The bed was unmade, and judging by the thin layer of dust, no one had been there in over twenty years.

I caught a glimpse of myself in the mirror, and I often wondered if I looked like my dad when he was my age. There weren't any pictures of him from that time, and it was hard to imagine Dad's face as younger, unlined, and free from worry or troubles. I had my mother's eyes, according to my dad, but everything else was his. At twenty years old, I was a couple of inches over six feet, and weighed a good two hundred pounds. Physically, I was a match for my father. That was what Mom had said. I took her at her word, since Dad always seemed much bigger.

The closet doorknob twisted slowly and I called out to Julia. "All clear!"

Julia opened the closet door and stepped out. She was a petite woman, blonde and blue eyed, with a quick laugh and bright smile. She was the object of attention wherever we went, and there were some times I think she might have started fights on purpose. Nevertheless, Julia was about as good a zombie fighter as you could hope for, and she had a knack for always finding what we were sent out for.

Julia looked around and seemed surprised that the room was clear of zombies. She stepped over to the window, looked out, and whistled softly.

"Nice work. Where did you come from, the stairwell?" She looked back at me.

"Nope. Came up from the floor below. Through the window." At her quizzical look, I shrugged. "Jake was blocking the door."

"Figures." Julia tossed her hair back and retied her ponytail. She went over to the corner and retrieved her weapon, a short handled spear with a long blade on one end and a metal knob on the other. When she started spinning with that thing, zombies tended to lose a lot of themselves.

"What happened?" I asked. I was rather put out that Julia hadn't actually thanked me for saving her butt, but maybe she would later.

"Got surprised, that's all. I thought there were some on the other side of the pocket door, but didn't figure they could get out." Julia shouldered her backpack and picked up a small duffle bag from the closet.

"Did you get what we needed?" I tried one more time to see if I might get a thank you, but I had a feeling, it was a lost cause.

Julia looked at me in an irritated manner. "Of course." She looked at the window. "You want to use the stairs or head out the way you came?"

I was starting to get angry, so I just said, "After you."

CHAPTER 2

Julia went to the back of the building where the stairs were. The kitchen was cluttered and in disarray, but had nothing we could use. Besides, any foodstuffs would likely kill us quicker than the zombies, just in a more painful manner. I wasn't a big fan of trying to crap myself to death.

At the stairwell, another zombie decided to make an appearance. This one was older, and had probably been in the house for a long time. It was a woman, and her threadbare clothing hung off her thin frame like a towel draped over a broomstick. Julia didn't even bother to slow down. She kicked the zombie down the stairs. I could hear the ghoul's bones cracking as it bounced and clattered down the steps.

We followed along, turning in time to see Jake rapping the zombie on the head with his mace.

"Here you are," Jake said to me. He looked at Julia. "You got what we need?"

"Right here, as usual," Julia said, lifting the duffle bag. She gave Jake a little smile and I was starting to feel a bit put out.

"All right. Let's get back. I want to be in the water by dark," Jake said, moving down the stairs.

I followed behind Julia, and to put it mildly, I was feeling a trifle angry. However, as usual, I bit down the thing I wanted to say and just stayed quiet. We moved to the first floor, and there were about fifty zombies milling about outside on the street. They were the ones that had followed us from the lakefront, and while we had reduced their numbers somewhat in the beginning, they were back up to full strength quickly. That wasn't hard to do, since the city had about a million or so zombies still walking around from the first days of the world's end.

Jake looked out the window and sized up the situation. "We can bust out of here pretty quickly, but we're going to have to distract them again. Aaron, why don't you make some noise out back?"

I looked at Jake for a second before I answered. "Why don't *you* make noise and *I'll* lead the way." I hadn't crossed Jake before on his leadership, so I surprised him with my response. To tell the truth, I surprised myself even more.

Jake slowly turned to face me. His brown eyes tended to look black when he was angry, and they were getting there right now. "I hate repeating myself, little brother. Go back to the rear of the goddamn house and make some noise."

I don't know what was coming over me, but suddenly I was icy calm, my breathing was slow and measured, and my eyes stared right back at Jake. "I heard you the first time, big brother, and I'm saying the same thing I said before, since you clearly are hard of hearing. *You* do it."

Green eyes fought with brown, and it would have gotten ugly, if Julia hadn't spoken up.

"Oh, for shit's sake. I'll do it. Try not to kill each other, you damn fools."

I watched Julia strolled to the back of the house, where she stopped in the kitchen to grab a pot and a wooden spoon. With a disgusted glance at the two of us, she went into the bathroom. A few seconds later, a clanging could be heard on the side of the house.

I turned back to Jake to find a knife in my face. Jake stared at me over the blade that was inches from my eyes.

"Never take your eyes off your enemy, *little* brother. You'll never survive if you keep screwing up." Jake smirked at me and moved the knife closer, bringing the point to within an inch of my eyes.

In a flash, I grabbed Jake's wrist, twisting the knife away with my left hand. My right hand grabbed his neck and with a shove, I slammed my brother into the wall. The doorframe smacked into the back of his hand and Jake dropped the knife. He clutched at my wrist with his free hand, but I wasn't about to let go. He tried kicking me, but I blocked the kick with a raised knee.

I moved my face to within few inches of Jake's. He was spitting mad, but couldn't do anything about it. I was taller than he was by several inches, and much stronger. Dad said Jake took after his mother while I took after him. I think I got the better end of the deal. I was tall, broad-shouldered and strong, while Jake was average sized and not as broad.

"I think I'll do fine. *Big* brother." I twisted suddenly, bringing Jake away from the wall and into the middle of the room. He stumbled as I let go and then turned to face me. His eyes were ugly and his mouth was twisted into a snarl.

"This isn't over." Jake stooped to pick up his knife and I kept a hand on my own as I waited for him to sheath it.

"It had better be," I said calmly. I couldn't believe the change that had come over me. Jake was usually able to bully me into doing what he wanted, but for some reason, I had had enough. However, I didn't underestimate Jake at all. I knew from experience and training that Jake, while not as large as me, was deadly with his hands and weapons. Our father had trained us for years, making sure we would be ready for anything that came our way. Julia's father had done the same with her. Our two dads were probably the deadliest zombie killers to come out of the end of the world. All of the lessons they had learned the hard way, they tried to repeatedly beat into our skulls. Jake took to the training differently than I did. During the last few years, he took more of an interest in not just besting the zombie, but destroying it. I took a more practical view, just get the thing down and out, and not worry about finessing it.

Jake stared at me some more, and when it became clear he wasn't going to try anything new, I turned away from him and looked out the window. Julia's banging had attracted a lot more zombies, but the ones that had been blocking the front had gone into the walkway and were no longer a threat. Trouble was coming, though, because the banging was going to attract a lot of zombies in a hurry that hadn't been here before.

Julia stopped and came running into the front. "Ready?" She looked to Jake who cocked an eyebrow at me.

"Lead the way," he said, hefting his mace. He smiled, but the smile didn't reach his eyes and I knew he was thinking of a way to get back at me. I didn't feel like having to watch my back the whole time, so I decided to throw him off a bit.

"On my way. And Jake?" I asked sweetly, moving towards the door.

"What now, Aaron? Get moving, will you?" Jake shifted impatiently.

"Did you even see me move?" With that question, I was out the door. I didn't see Jake's reaction, but I would bet a silver that he was thinking about it and wasn't happy.

CHAPTER 3

I ran down the steps of the home and out into the street. We didn't have far to go, but it was that short distance, which was going to be trouble. Dozens of zombies were in the streets, and as I burst out onto the scene, they were nearly frantic. Some of them probably hadn't seen food in years, outside of the occasional rat they managed to catch.

Julia was right behind me, with Jake following her. We ran in a shifting pattern, from one side of the street to the other, keeping the zombies off track. They couldn't shift as well as we could, and the direction changes really tossed their minds about. We couldn't avoid all of them, so some needed to be killed as they came too close. The problem was that we couldn't stop our movement and finish them properly, because we'd get swamped in a hurry.

One zombie was slightly faster than I anticipated, and he lurched in front of me. I jumped slightly and kicked it squarely in the chest. The zombie went flying and I kept moving. Julia barely slowed down, while Jake actually took the time to kill the thing.

"What the hell are you doing?" hissed Julia as she looked back.

Jake trotted up smiling. "What needs to be done."

I said nothing, as I kept moving, because I knew he was doing everything he could to level some criticism at me. Jake was like that these days. He would poke and poke and poke, and when you had enough, he would challenge you to do something about it, trusting he could handle whatever you threw at him. I ignored a lot of it, but lately, it had been getting on my nerves.

We ran for about two blocks, and then ducked into an alleyway to catch our breath. Nothing was chasing us that could catch us at the present, but all it took was one to see us and we would be trapped.

While we breathed quietly, I took a second to look at our map. Our boat was on the river, but we would be crazy to run back the way we came. The zombies that had chased us in were likely still waiting for us to return, so to go back into their loving embrace was something I'd say we needed to avoid. The map had several routes we could take, but the problem was that we had zombies everywhere, and they were stirred up. It was as if they knew something was different, and they were out to see what it was.

We were about to head back out when a zombie suddenly stumbled into the alleyway entrance. He took a second to size us up, and I could almost see his eyes widen and his nostrils flare, taking in the treats before him. He was an ugly piece of work, with deep black gashes across his face and chest. One eye was stuck looking down, while the other gazed at us.

His hand reached out slowly, as if to see if we were actually real, and I took that opportunity to grab his hand and pull him into the alley. I yanked him past me and kicked him in the seat of the pants as he went by. He stumbled to the ground and as he was on his hands and knees getting up, Jake cracked his skull with his mace.

"Any more?" Julia said. She had just watched the whole thing, figuring my brother and I would handle it.

I snuck a quick peek out into the street and while there were a lot, none were paying any attention to our particular location.

"Not nearby, but it's going to get tricky closer to the water," I said, watching Jake for his reaction.

Surprisingly, he nodded. "The ones we left behind will probably be waiting. Any suggestions?"

"Just one. The buildings here are the same size for the next three blocks. Let's get on the roof, so we don't have to worry about the ones on the ground, and we can avoid the ones hanging out inside," I said.

They mulled it over for a second, and I thought they were going to argue, but then their minds were made up for them. At the entrance to the alleyway, about five gruesome looking specimens walked into view, and as soon as they saw us, a hideous, wheezing groan came from about three of them. It was hard to tell what they had been in real life, but there was no mistaking what they were now.

"Back! Get to the dumpster!" Jake shoved Julia ahead of him and followed closely behind, running to a dark green garbage bin in the corner of the alley. I was right behind him, and when we reached the dumpster, we both squatted down and heaved the thing onto its side. That little maneuver raised the height of the bin another two feet, and the side of the bin was much more stable than the lid or the wheels.

Jake helped Julia up and she in turn pulled him up. The two of them pulled me up, and I then shoved Julia up and over the lip of the roof. I cupped my hands for Jake and he placed his foot in, being launched skyward when I straightened.

I spun around and leapt for the roof, catching it with my hands and hanging precariously for a minute. The zombies had reached the dumpster and were now looking upward, reaching with hands, their mouths gaping. If I fell now, I'd be easily killed.

"Little help?" I called, and Julia was right there, grabbing my wrist and pulling as much as she could. Try as she might, though, she didn't have the strength. Trouble was, the roof edge was very smooth, so I was having a hard time holding on.

"Jake! Get over here!" Julia called.

I couldn't see him, but I hoped he was getting closer, as my arms were getting tired.

Jake's face appeared above me and he looked down contemptuously. "My head still hurts, asshole." His face disappeared and Julia yelled at him.

"Jake!"

Fuck him. I thought. I did a pull-up, even though my arms were starting to burn, and I managed to hook an arm over the side of the roof. I swung a leg up and was able to get a foot over the edge, easing the weight off my arms. Twisting over, I fell onto my side and back, my melee weapon jabbing me painfully in the back.

CHAPTER 4

I lay there for a minute, catching my breath. Julia knelt down by my head with what looked like real concern in her eyes. It was nice to see, actually. I smiled at her and held up a finger, slowing my breathing down and easing the tension in my arms.

Jake walked over and looked at me. "Hmm. Pity. I was hoping to get an apology before I helped you."

Julia stood up and rounded on Jake. "He's your brother, you shit! What if he had lost his grip? What if we both had gone over because I was trying to pull him up?"

Jake looked at her for a minute before replying. "That would have been a problem," he admitted.

I stood up, not wanting to be on the ground anymore, and watched as Julia growled and punched Jake in the chest. The punch was hard enough to elicit a noise from Jake, and then Julia stalked off to the other side of the roof to see about getting across.

I walked over to Jake and he looked up at me. "I wouldn't have let you fall, baby brother."

I stared hard at Jake, trying to control myself. When I replied, it was barely above a whisper. "I wish I could believe you, *brother*." I fairly spat the last word at him and walked away, too angry to trust myself to stay in his vicinity.

I went over to Julia and looked over the roof. The alley was about six feet wide, but the problem was the other roof had what amounted to a fence, just like this side.

"Any thoughts? We can't just jump, because we'd have to clear both barricades." Julia looked around, and shrugged.

"I could toss you, but you'd probably break an ankle on landing, so that's out, and Jake sure as hell wouldn't trust me to throw him," I said.

"Rope?" Julia suggested, pointing to the pipes and vents coming out of the roof.

"How do we get to the other side to tie it off?" I asked, trying to figure out a way.

"How about you two grow a set and do it the easy way?" Jake put a discarded five-gallon bucket about three feet from the roof ledge, and stepped back about fifteen feet.

Curious, I wondered how he was going to pull this off. At the moment, I kind of hoped he was going to fall and break his stupid neck.

Jake ran forward, stepping once on the bucket, then on the edge of the roof. He sailed over the opening, and landed heavily on the other side. A second later, he popped up and grinned, looking very much like the Jake I used to know.

"Coming?" He asked.

Julia looked at me and shrugged. She stepped back to where Jake had started his run, and then took off. She flew to the other side, landing and rolling. Jake helped her to her feet, and then they both looked at me.

"All right. Why not?" I repeated the procedure, but when I landed, I skidded to a stop, staying on my feet the whole time. I cocked an eyebrow at Jake, who nodded in appreciation.

"I'll have to do a flip to top that one," Jake said, moving to the other side of the roof. Fortunately, the buildings for the next five businesses were right up against each other, so we were able to cover an entire block without touching the street.

When we reached the street, we looked over and it wasn't a good thing. There were about fifty zombies wandering about, and probably twice that many hanging about indoors. When the end of the world was a few years old, some of the zombies started to learn a few things, especially when it came to their survival. The big thing was they didn't spend as much time outdoors, hanging about inside and mostly staring at the walls. They would come out for a meal, though, no question about that, and if something got their attention; but otherwise, there were a lot of nasty surprises when you were out hunting for things.

"What now?" Jake asked, looking over the edge. He was on his stomach so the zombies couldn't see him, but he had a good view of the street.

I was right next to him and I shrugged. "I guess we could lob a timer out there, and hope like hell it stays intact enough to go off."

Jake mulled it over. "We could. We'd have to be ready to go in a second, and be able to get up on the next roof."

"Timing is everything. What if we can't get up in time?" Julia asked. "We had five on us in a hurry last time, and out there is quite a few more."

"Anything we can use up here?" I asked, looking around. The roof was fairly clear of debris, except for the occasional ball and bottle. We sometimes found guns on roofs, remnants of a time when criminals would ditch their weapons by tossing them up on a roof. No gun, no conviction.

Jake looked over the side again. "There's nothing to prop up against the side. Wait! Over there by that back fence!" Jake pointed towards the back of the building across the street and in the alleyway that formed the access road for the homes behind the businesses was a pile of lumber and fence pieces.

"Nice." I said. "Anything look long enough for the roof?"

"Even if it's five feet short, it's still long enough," Jake replied.

"All right, but how do we all get up at the same time?" I normally didn't play devil's advocate, but I really did want to be sure I was on that roof fairly quickly.

"Depends on what we find. Come on, we're losing daylight, and I really don't want to spend another night in the city." Jake said, back crawling and taking off his backpack to find a noisemaker.

I couldn't blame him for that sentiment. We had spent enough nights in the city as it was, and each time, it got worse. The ghouls came out in force, hunting and searching, and if they caught the scent of you or heard you, there was no place to go. They also groaned all night long, which was extremely irritating.

CHAPTER 5

Jake pulled out a small timer, and wound it up to five minutes. He placed it in a rusty coffee can, and stepping as close as he dared to the edge of the roof, he tossed it as far as he could. Julia and I were already climbing down the back of the building before Jake even threw.

We heard the clang of the can and the zombies immediately set up a groan. Jake slipped over the side of the building and hung for a second, dropping down and pulling off his mace. I wasn't ready to pull out my big melee weapon yet, but I had no problems with my tomahawk. It was a nice, one solid piece of metal from blade to lanyard loop. The beard was sharpened as well as the main blade, and the spike had been sharpened along the top edge. Julia's dad had given it to me, and with it, the instructions on how to use it. I could throw it reasonably accurately up to thirty yards, and could kill easily using it with either hand.

Julia pulled the sheath off the blade on her staff and gave a nod. I nodded to Jake and we crept quietly to the corner of the building. I checked several times to make sure there was no one in the alley with us. That mistake had cost more than one person their lives.

A minute later, the timer went off, echoing loudly out of the can. It worked very well, drawing all of the zombies in the immediate vicinity away to the front of the building.

"Go! Go! Go!" Jake whispered, sprinting across the street. Julia and I were right behind him and we all flew across the small street into the back of the building. Jake wasted no time, diving into the lumber and grabbing a long two by twelve. It was about ten feet long, with a crack along one side and a full complement of bugs on the other.

"Ewwww! Julia whispered as she grabbed one end of the board. She hated bugs.

"Suck it up, they're on their way!" Jake hissed, yanking the board over to the building. He was talking about the zombies that we ran in front of to get over here. There weren't many, but if they delayed us and got us noticed by the rest, we were in trouble.

Jake and Julia leaned the board against the wall and Julia scampered up it. It bent slightly in the middle, but it didn't crack. Jake went next, but I didn't have time to watch him go, since a rather ugly zombie came stumbling out of the street. He was once an overweight man and had died wearing a really loud Hawaiian shirt. The left side of his face and neck were completely gone, as if someone had grabbed hold of his nose and pulled backwards really fast.

I waited until he was close enough, and then I dispatched him with a quick spike to the head. Three more were on their way, and I could see several others becoming interested in the street gymnastics.

"Aaron! Up!" Jake called from the roof. He was holding Julia's spear, and was waiting to lend a hand. I guess he had gotten over the events in the house, and was ready to make nice. Either that, or Julia had a knife in his ribs I couldn't see.

I put my axe back in its sheath on my thigh and spun for the board. Two steps up and the thing began to crack. Another step and it cracked loudly, and I knew it wasn't going to hold my weight.

"Jump!" Jake yelled and I launched myself up just as the board cracked and split. I managed to grab the ball end of the staff and held on for dear life.

"Hang on!" Jake levered the staff over the edge of the roof and pulled down, bending the shaft quite a bit, but the ash handle held and I was able to swing a leg up and over the roof.

I stepped off the edge and caught my breath. "Thanks, Jake," I said.

"No problem, thank God you're not fat." Jake grinned. Despite myself, I did actually like my brother from time to time.

"Let's go, guys, we've got a mile to go and almost no daylight left," Julia warned, heading for the other side of the buildings.

She was right, and it looked like we might not make it even then. If that happened, we had some problems.

We reached the next street, and got lucky in that most of the zombies were far enough down the road that we were able to drop off the roof, get Julia on the next roof, then lower a rope for Jake and myself. We got up and were on our way before they had a chance to get even halfway to us.

At the end of the next building, we had a bit of a dilemma. We needed to get off the roof and head for the river, and we were about a half mile from where we needed to be.

"Any thoughts?" Julia asked.

"The only upside is the dusk. They can't see us too well, but that doesn't matter if enough of them do." Jake said, looking over the terrain. We had to run through two blocks of high-rises, then get down to the river where our boat was.

"Do we have anything we can distract them with?" I asked, receiving shakes of heads in response.

"What if we set a fire?" Julia asked. We had done that in the past, and it worked up to a point, but we usually did it in the day. At night, the flames would call in every zombie for a mile or more.

"Too risky now." I said. "I'm thinking with time being short, we need to just run for it, dodge and go. No killing." I looked pointedly at Jake and he had the grace to grin slightly.

"All right. I'll take point and Julia, you take the center. Aaron, you're our backup if we need help," Jake said.

Julia and I nodded, and we readied our weapons. Julia hefted her spear and checked the haft to see if there was any damage from Jake using it as a lever. I pulled out my 'hawk and knife, adjusting my grip on both. The knife was a big bladed bowie knife, with a coffin-handled ebony grip. My Uncle Tom had given it to me as a kind of joke, but the blade was all business. Twelve inches of sharpened carbon steel would cut the leg off a zombie with no trouble. Jake choked up on his mace and pulled out his knife again. His blade was smaller, but it was curved more, and designed more for penetration than cutting, although it did the latter extremely well.

"Let's rock it. Last one to the boat has to paddle," Jake said.

"You're on," said Julia. She could never turn down a challenge.

"See you two later." I slid down the drainpipe from the roof and waited for the other two to get down. When Jake hit the ground, we were off.

CHAPTER 6

Jake ran down the center of the street, with Julia and me right behind him. We ran full tilt, not giving the zombies a chance to identify us fully before we were gone. A chorus of groans followed in our wake, and in a short amount of time, we had a huge following of zombies, eager to rip us to shreds.

The first block wasn't too bad, we only had a few to dodge around. The next block was a little worse, because the zombies were alerted to something going on and were facing us as we ran towards them. Jake started dodging from one side to the other, and it was difficult keeping up. However, I knew what he was trying to do, and that was to keep the zombies from zeroing in on us and cutting us off.

Jake ran over a car, dodging a pocket of zombies, and by the time I got there, I had to jump over a couple of grasping arms.

I nearly slipped on the windshield while stepping down, and my curse caused Julia to look back. She slipped on a dead body on the ground and nearly fell. Fortunately, I was right behind her and caught her before she hit the ground. I actually carried her for a few steps before she got her feet under her.

"Thanks!" she panted, taking off again. She looked at me kind of funny when I ran with her, as if she was surprised, I carried her so easily. Truth was she didn't weigh that much, and I was fairly strong, so I didn't think anything of it.

"Come on, it's just a bit farther!" Jake said, ducking under an outstretched arm. Julia and I ran around the same zombie on the other side, causing that former woman to spin in place and fall on her butt.

We reached the edge of the river, but we weren't out of the woods yet. We still had to get down to the riverside and launch our boat. Behind us, about two thousand zombies were lurching along the street, with more pouring out of buildings and shops. We had to get moving in the boat and get moving fast. Add to that, the darkness had seriously fallen, and the shadows of the skyscrapers made things darker than they normally would have been out in the open.

We raced down a flight of stairs, passing the restaurant that was normally our landing point for excursions into this part of the city. Back in the day, it would have been a neat place to eat, but now it was just a memory with faded tables and broken windows.

At the landing, Julia climbed into the boat and secured the duffle bag while Jake worked at the rope. I stood at the top of the stairs leading down to the landing, and I had the great job of watching the hordes tumble down the stairs and groan with rare enthusiasm. I wouldn't doubt some of these zombies were original leftovers from the very beginning of the apocalypse.

As I stood there, I waited for Jake to get the rope untied. I could see him struggling, and I called down to see what the matter was. In a minute, I was going to have my hands very full.

"Come on, Jake! They're almost here!" I shifted, but I couldn't move just yet.

"I'm trying, but the damn thing got pulled tight somehow and it's not letting go!" Jake sounded genuinely panicked, so I knew he wasn't horsing around. I could hear Julia adding her two cents to hurry as well.

Seven zombies, the advance guard of the Chicago Horde, came stumbling through the riverside patio portion of the restaurant. I had just a few seconds before it was over.

"Jake!"

"Trying! One minute!"

"I haven't got a minute. Aw, hell."

CHAPTER 7

"Aaron!" Julia could see what was coming and could do nothing to help.

Jake looked up and he was about to let go of the rope when I called down.

"Stay there!" Suddenly I was calm. While I had been panicky before, I was deadly calm now. I put my tomahawk away and sheathed my knife. I reached a hand back and pulled out my heavy fighting weapon. It was a single-edged sword with a wide blade and a half-inch thick spine. The edge swept up to a point that could punch through a piece of sheet metal with ease. The hilt was designed for using with a single hand, but a second could be employed easily for increased cutting power. My Uncle Duncan had given it to me a couple of years ago, calling it a 'falchion', but it was a butcher's blade and little else. He spent hours training me with it, telling me that the odds of me fighting someone else with a sword was really rare, so we focused on cutting, proper stance, and effective follow-through.

The first hands that reached for me, I cut off at the wrist, pivoting to the side and delivering a horizontal cut that removed the head of the zombie as well. I stepped forward and delivered a low cut that swept through the knees of two zombies, dropping them to the ground. They still tried to get up, but failed badly. I brought the sword up in a high arc, cutting through a zombie's neck and torso, removing the shoulder and arm as well. I swung the sword around and cut the top two inches off the next one in line, killing him instantly. The next three charged and I just went to town, slashing as quickly as I could, tossing zombie parts all over the place. In a few short seconds, I was alone again, although there were more of them coming down the stairs.

"How's it going, Jake?" I asked, stepping down the stairs to the landing. My big blade was in my hand, dripping zombie gore. Both Julia and Jake looked at me as if I was some sort of medieval nightmare, although Julia had that same odd kind of look on her face.

"Jesus, Aaron," Jake said. "You just killed seven zombies in like, what, five seconds?"

"That long?" I tried to be funny, but I was still jacked on adrenaline. I stepped into the boat and flicked the blade at the rope, cutting it neatly below the knot that Jake had so much trouble with. The boat slid away into the water and Jake didn't bring up the point that technically, I should be paddling.

I took out a small bottle of kerosene from my pack, and squirted a decent amount of the fluid on the blade, I still held unsheathed. Julia had a lighter handy, and she lit my sword. Red flames burned brightly, illuminating the tall, dead buildings that flanked us as we rode down the river. I held my sword aloft as a reminder to the dead that they still had a master.

The flames sputtered and slowly died out, and I stuck my sword into the water to quench any leftover flames. After letting it dry, I sheathed it and picked up a paddle, adding to Jake's strokes and getting us away from the city one more time.

The river's edge was lined with dead people, and they stared with a curious intensity as we passed. The virus had affected some in the weird way that made their eyes glow in the dark, and it was always creepy to see floating lights move in the dark areas and know they were attached to some dead thing. Groans echoed around the building canyons and I always listened to see if there was ever any change on pitch that indicated a zombie on the hunt. Low groans meant they were just making noise. Higher pitched groans meant they had spotted their prey, and groans bordering on snarls meant they were closing in and about to kill.

I don't know why I bothered. It wasn't like we were going to stop and help anyway. Too many people had been killed helping like that, and we had learned our lessons at the feet of the masters. We can't save them all was the first lesson we learned after gaining some skill as fighters. Don't bother trying.

After a while, we passed the outer edges and started to see the buildings start to lose some height. It was the first sign that we were passing out of the city. We passed by a burned out hospital, and Jake always looked up to the building, as if he was seeking something, or something was calling him. I never asked, and he never explained. This time, I wondered if it had something to do with the mood he was in, why he was angry all the time. I would have to ask him once we were home and then pick a time when he was far away from pointy things.

CHAPTER 8

We spent the night in an abandoned house on the other side of the Wall. When the end of the world happened, my father and several others realized the threat from the zombies in the city would never stop causing problems unless they were contained. Over the course of several months and the loss of a lot of lives, a barrier was erected around the city. It wasn't anything fancy, just cargo containers, boxcars, and sheet metal welded together, but it worked at keeping the zombies in and the curious out.

People still went in, danger seekers who got tired of living, or teenagers daring each other to make a zombie run. It didn't matter the reason, it was dangerous as hell. Once upon a time, there was a fad of proving oneself by spending a night in the city. Julia's father put an end to that in a hurry. He told the kids that if they wanted to prove themselves, pick up a knife and come at him. If they lived, they were proven. No one took him up on the offer.

In the suburbs, on the south side of the wall, there were still thousands of uninhabited houses. Most of them had been systematically looted of anything useful or valuable, but they were free of zombies and kept you out of the rain and wind.

A few minutes before dawn, I woke up on the floor in the bedroom. It was something I had done for years, and my dad always told me it was lucky to be able to do it. Jake, on the other hand, slept as if he just discovered it, and it took a lot to get that man out of bed.

I got up off the floor and looked out the window, down the empty street and across the sea of empty homes. It would have been a decent thing to burn the whole area down, but this close to the Wall meant a breach might occur, and then we would be right back where we started.

I spent a moment running a whetstone over the edge of my sword and knife, and then put my gear on in practiced moves. I thought about heading home today, and found myself to be impatient to get there. Not sure why, since there wasn't anything for me there outside of my relatives and cousins, but it was home, none the less.

Julia surprised me by being awake early. She was in the kitchen area using a small bowl she had found and was washing her face and arms, trying to clean up as best she could. She could have turned on a faucet, but guessing what might come out would stump even the best of psychics.

"Oh! Aaron! You startled me!" Julia jumped slightly when she opened her eyes after drying out the water.

'Sorry." I said, noting a drop of water hung tenaciously to her chin. It was a nice chin, I decided. I wasn't really sure why I noticed, I had known Julia my entire life and basically she was my sister, but I did notice, anyway. "How did you sleep?"

"As well as usual, when I'm not at home," Julia replied. "Too many noises I'm not used to."

"That's for sure," I said. I changed the subject. "Anything for breakfast?" I asked, opening up a couple of cabinet drawers and peering in.

"You can try your luck with the unlabeled cans in the pantry." Julia suggested, with a slight twinkle in her eyes.

I laughed, because that was another game we used to play growing up. Someone would find a can, and we would first lay bets on what might be inside, then lay bets as to who would try and eat a bite. Afterwards, we would quietly lay bets as to whether the taster would actually survive. If you were a good guesser, you could make some decent money. You might lose a friend or two, but you'd have money.

"No thanks. Anytime I think about that or am tempted to give it a try, I remember Bill Tract and the chili." I said, smiling.

Julia laughed. "Oh, God! I remember that! He was lucky to survive at all."

I nodded. Bill Tract took a single bite of what amounted to eighteen-year-old chili in a can. In one minute, he was puking his guts out. While he was bending over retching, his bowels let go and he shit himself sideways. Two weeks and twenty pounds later, he was finally able to stand on his own.

"I'll stick with the corn biscuits." I said, digging through my pack. Corn biscuits were homemade corn meal balls compressed and dried, then packed dry. You typically broke them up and dropped them in a cup of water, and ate the resulting mush. With a little salt, they were actually pretty decent. If you didn't have any water, you could put some in your mouth and gnaw on it for about three hours.

Julia finished her washing, and after ordering me to turn around, put on a fresh t-shirt. She packed up her stuff, and then put her gear on, too. When she finished, she came over and stood by me, staring intently at me with big blue eyes until I relented and gave her a biscuit. Some things never changed. She used to do this when we were kids, too.

Julia and I enjoyed a quiet moment, just eating and looking out the windows when a loud thumping came from the upstairs. My adrenaline rushed slightly before I realized we were on the outside of the Wall, and the thumping wasn't a zombie, it was Jake.

Julia and I shared a look, and said the same thing together.

"Jake's up."

Jake was a grumpy riser, and if he slept hard enough, he might forget where he was. If that was the case, things might get very interesting, very soon. Julia must have been reading my mind, because she suddenly clapped a hand to her mouth.

"Do you think he'll do it?" She asked.

"Only if he's half awake, and the layout is the same." I said, thinking about it.

"I was laughing so hard the last time that I peed my pants," Julia said, giggling.

I moved away slightly. "Thanks for the warning."

Julia punched me on the arm, and we stood quietly, waiting to see if Jake would be sleepy enough to use the toilet. Plumbing systems relied on gravity and these systems had degraded from lack of use over the years. If you flushed one of the 'lost johns' the dry-rotted fixtures usually gave up, sending foul water everywhere. Jake did that once before and wound up smelling like a sewer for a week. I got a month's worth of teasing material from that episode. Even our dad thought it was hilarious.

The thumping sounds continued and we watched the ceiling to see if history would repeat itself.

Suddenly, there was a loud bang, and a heartfelt "Ow! Dammit, who the hell put that there?" Followed by a calmer, "Oh, wait. Not my house."

Julia and I shared a look. Our fun wouldn't be happening today. It sounded like Jake had knocked himself fully awake. Of course, that meant he was going to be grumpy about bumping into something.

Ten minutes later, Jake thumped down the stairs, carrying his backpack, weapons, and a serious grouch. He dumped the gear on the floor, while he went out the back door. The yards in the suburbs had grown so much they had become a forest, with homes hidden in the brush. Two steps off the porch, Jake had effectively disappeared.

Five minutes later, Jake came back. He seemed to be in a better mood, and took a moment to wash off his face and rinse out the sleep from his eyes.

"Well, that wasn't too bad," Jake said to no one in particular, referring to the events of the last two days.

"Not really," I replied. I wasn't too talkative as a rule, and didn't feel the need to start changing that trait now.

"Never saw you use that blade so well before," Jake said, eyeing the hilt that stuck up over my right shoulder. "I've seen you cut apart a lone zombie, but that group thing was pretty amazing.'

"I do what I need to," I said casually. On the outside, I was calm, but inside I was a bit nervous. Besides my dad, I always wanted to have Jake's approval. I wasn't sure why, but maybe it was because he was my big brother. We were equal fighters, with different strengths and weaknesses, but I still felt a need for Jake to think well of me.

"You did great," Julia said. Jake glanced her way while I smiled at her. It meant a lot to have Julia's approval, too, but it wasn't quite the same.

"Plan for today?" I asked, changing the subject. I was never comfortable as the center of attention.

"Finish our business and be on our way. See if there's any more jobs for us, and if not, head for home." Jake said, taking a bite of his own biscuit, and then wetting it down with his canteen. He'd keep that chunk of biscuit in his cheek for a while.

"All right then," I said. "Let's get moving."

CHAPTER 9

We grabbed our stuff and Jake showed me a handful of gold and silver jewelry he had found in a hidden place in the house. I nodded in approval, thinking this trip was already profitable, and Jake's find was making a good thing better. Hopefully the Melting Pot will be open today at the capital.

We walked the short distance from the house to the canal and climbed into our canoe. I pushed us off the side of the canal and we slipped quietly into the water. I guided us out to the edge of the shadows, experience teaching us that while we took our own risks for our business, others weren't so brave. They were, however, willing to steal your treasures if they got the chance. Most of the time, we were left alone, but we never stopped being cautious. A competing group did attack us once on this route, but Julia sliced the hell out of the leader before the attack was fully underway, and the rest lost their nerve after seeing how much blood the human body could lose if opened correctly.

The riverbanks were well grown with trees and brush. Many trees had branches that touched the water, narrowing the usable part of the channel and creating underwater hazards. Fortunately, our canoe was aluminum, so we were pretty safe unless we hit something metallic or rocky.

The mist on the water parted for us, swirling in time with the whorls on the water as we moved quietly by, disappearing as we travelled west. Little blips of water betrayed curious fish, and cranes hunted the shallows in side canals and channels. Here and there rusted forms slowly disintegrated by the water's edge, remnants of a time when the world was very different.

We had been down this canal several times before, and I could point out numerous reference spots that I used to mark our passage. Some were safe harbors, some were good hunting grounds, and others were good fishing grounds. A couple were places to avoid, as people moved away from population centers to start their own towns, they had different notions about what laws to enforce. When our dad was around, these places couldn't have existed. Now, they seemed to be popping up more often. One such place, Zoomertown, it was called, built itself right up to the Wall. They were fairly lawless, and was a good place to go if you were looking for trouble. A lot of youngsters from the capital came up that way to get their first drink, sleep with their first whore, and look at their first zombie. You had to have money though, and it was rumored that someone died every week from a knife wound or a bad drink. A lot of kids didn't come back, and it was rumored that agents from Zoomertown roamed the capital, looking for young girls to steal. When we passed these places, Jake would put down his paddle and pick up his rifle until we were clear.

Once we cleared the heaviest of the suburbs, I could see the capital lands. Soon we would be passing the orchards and the grazing lands, and finally, the farmlands for the capital.

Around mid-morning, we reached the outskirts of Leport, the capital of the New United States. In the twenty years since its renaming, the population had grown from several hundred to tens of thousands. Dad had said it was one of the few places around, which looked like a city used to look. None of us had any clue what he was talking about. Going to the capital as kids used to be such a treat. We would ride up the river, waving at the stray zombies on the canal edges, coming up to see old friends and play with new ones. We would see a movie and go to dinner, and spend some time with people our fathers called the 'old guard.' They would talk about the Zombie Wars; drink to fallen friends, and in a couple of days, head back for home. The capital now, for us, was a place to do business. Lately, it was trouble, too.

At the docks, we slipped into a small opening and Jake tied off his end while I took care of mine. I helped Julia out and she carefully pulled up the duffle bag that carried our precious cargo, the thing we went through miles of zombie territory for. We left our heavy melee weapons in the boat; they'd be safe until we returned.

Walking up the dock and onto the street, we threw waves to people who knew us, had known our parents, or had done business with us. Several people looked us over, unused to the gear we were wearing and the weapons we were carrying. They knew what we were, but seeing one of us up close was different.

"Lots of new faces," Jake said, looking over at a group of men standing outside a wine-seller's place. One man noticed Julia and jostled another, causing that one to notice her as well. Both men openly stared until we passed from view. Julia couldn't help herself. She was, for lack of a better word, stunning. She was also completely oblivious; her attention was always focused on the children that ran around the town. She loved kids and they loved to be with her. She was a natural mother; caring, compassionate, and fiercely protective.

"Yeah," I said, looking at the men, who stared back defiantly until we rounded the corner. "Let's get done and get home."

"Sounds good," Jake said. "You guys get the business done, I'll see the Melter and check to see if there is any new business worth looking at. I'll meet you back here in an hour." Jake turned down a side street and was off without another word.

I looked down at Julia and she shrugged. Jake was like that, and there was no changing him.

CHAPTER 10

"What's the address?" I asked, looking up at the homes on the hills. I hoped it would be a short walk.

Julia looked at the piece of paper attached to the duffle bag. "Says here that it's up on fourth, on the other side of the cemetery."

I thought a minute, and then groaned. "Damn. It's up the hill and another half mile walk besides."

Julia started walking. "Never knew you disliked exercise."

I followed a second later. "I dislike *extra* exercise," I said, defending myself. I kept up, but also kept an eye on our surroundings. The habit that served me well in our excursions, and did well when we were in supposedly friendlier territory.

We walked up the hill, rounding the bend in front of the old school that was used as a legislative building. Congress wasn't in session right now, so the building was quiet and had minimal activity. Supposedly, the original Constitution and Bill of Rights were housed within, but I hadn't seen them myself.

At Fourth Street, we walked over a small ditch and past a small grassy rise. The little hill was about four feet high, but combined with the ditch; the barrier was actually over eight feet. Once upon a time, Julia's dad had helped build that barricade to keep out the zombies that had been all over the place. Now it was a place kids played in and others cursed for its inconvenience. It was funny how quickly people forgot the effort that went into trying to save the world from extinction.

Two small rights and then a left found us standing in the door of a small, yet cozy home. Leport was like that. There were big homes, and right next door, there were little homes. People tended to go where their tastes and their egos took them. When the power was off, people stayed in the small houses because they were easier to heat in the winters. When the power came back on, there was a bit of a scramble for the bigger homes. These days, things seem to have settled down.

Julia knocked on the door and a small, older woman answered the door.

"Yes? Can I help you?" She asked. She looked at me a little apprehensively, and then kept her eyes on Julia.

"Ma'am? We're the collectors you hired. We found what you were looking for." Julia opened up the duffle bag and pulled out two large books. One looked like a photo album, and the other looked to be an ordinary book. She handed them over to the woman, who surprised me by suddenly tearing up and crying.

The woman held the books tightly and didn't say a word for a moment. "You got them. I thought they were gone forever. I can't believe you got them." She just kept saying it over and over again, tears falling off her face and splashing on the front porch.

Julia smiled and put her hand on the woman's shoulder, which seemed to shake her out of her moment.

"Oh, my God! You did it! I can't thank you enough! Oh, God! Charles will be so surprised. Charles! Come up here! I have a surprise for you!" The woman called into the house and then turned back to Julia and myself. "Thank you so much!" She hugged Julia and gave my arm a squeeze, her teary eyes filling with joy.

"We lost so much when we fled, and I thought we'd never get anything we had back, not after the city had been closed. Thank you again." The woman was nearly delirious, and I think I understood why Jake tended to avoid this part of the job.

"What is it, Maggie? Why are you crying? Jesus, you're huge!" A middle-aged man stepped into the doorway, sporting a very balding head and a bright shock of red hair bursting from above his ears. His big hands and arms told of years of hard work, while his bulging belly spoke of marrying a good cook. His last comment was aimed at me, and his eyes took me in at a glance, noting my shoulders and arms, and running a practiced eye over my weapons. If I had to guess, Charles here could handle a zombie or three without too much trouble.

Maggie handed Charles the book, and whatever I was expecting, it certainly wasn't to see Charles take the book like it was a newborn, and suddenly fall on his knees. He looked at the book for a long time, and then he slowly brought the book to his chest. He held it there for a long moment, and then stood up with difficulty.

When Charles was up, there were tears in his eyes as well. He kept looking at the book, then looking at us. He was so choked up he could barely speak.

"Thank you. May God bless your days forever," he said. Without another word, he went into the house and we could hear small sobs coming from within.

Maggie smiled at us and explained. "This is the photo album of our family from the time we were married. All of our pictures and memories are here. All of our good memories, anyway." Her eyes grew sad for a moment, but it quickly passed. "That other book is Charles' family bible, which was brought over from Ireland over a hundred years ago. That bible *is* his family, and his place in the world. You've no idea what you've brought back to us. Thank you."

Julia smiled. "You're very welcome. I hate to be awkward, but we did have a few expenses, and we will need the other half of our agreement?"

Maggie put a hand to her mouth. "Oh, of course! Where are my manners? Good heavens! I'll be right back!" She went into the house and a few minutes later Charles came out. His eyes were red but he was smiling.

"Maggie says to pay what we owe. Here it be, and my thanks to you both." Charles held out a small purse, and Julia took it gently, putting it in her vest pocket.

"Thank you, sir, and if you have any friends who might need something collected...?"

"I'll be sending them your way, no worries, lass." Charles, who originally didn't have an accent when he first showed up at the door, had developed a bit of an Irish tilt to his voice.

I shook his hand and we left the home, walking back the way we came. Julia and I basked in the feeling of a job well done, and once we were out of sight, she pulled out the purse.

"What's up?" I asked. "Something wrong? I can't believe Charles would short us."

"No, it's not that, it just feels funny; like it weighs too much." Julia pulled out the purse and opened it. Reaching in, she pulled out the coins and gasped. Instead of our final payment of five silver coins, Charles had replaced two of the silvers with gold coins.

I whistled when I saw the flash of gold. "Damn! If Jake even gets two for the stuff he found, we're doing well."

Julia nodded and put the money back into her vest. "Do you think he'll find another job?"

"Probably. There's always work for the likes of us," I said, hopping over the ditch and climbing the small hill. "Everyone loves the collectors."

CHAPTER 11

Collectors. That's what we were. We went out and collected the memories, the artifacts, the remnants of lives left behind when the world suddenly ended. People who had fled their homes way back when began to have a hankering for the things that defined them. We collected books, curios, keepsakes, and heirlooms. Stuff that had to be left behind became accessible once again. It all came down to who was willing to go for it and who was willing to pay to have it done. We charged ten silver coins for a job, five in advance and five when it was finished. We charged extra for longer distances, and reserved the right to refuse a job after we began, for an expense fee of two silvers. We never had to do that, but Jake said it made sure the people who sent us out knew they could lose out if it was a wild goose chase.

Over the last three years, we must have made a couple of dozen trips to the city, and a few trips out of state. We had made trips across the lake a couple of times, and went as far south as Texas, once. We wouldn't do that one again.

Other people trained for various jobs, like blacksmiths, plumbers, electricians, and so forth. From the time we were able to fight, we trained on how to handle zombies and how to survive far from help. Our fathers taught us to think on our feet, fight like the devil, and stay alive. Our mothers gave us our education, and I doubt there was a book within fifty miles of our home that we hadn't read.

We walked down the hill, feeling pretty good about ourselves, when the first hints of trouble began. The back of my neck started to prickle and I distinctly got the feeling we were being watched. Around the corner, I sized up the street and figured the best place for an ambush would be before we reached the storefronts. A house was there that looked abandoned, but as I learned very early, looks were often deceiving.

Julia's dad always taught us that if we thought we were walking into a trap, to turn around and run the other way. It confused the hell out of your ambushers. Julia was happily walking along when I put my arm around her waist. She stiffened and looked up at me, but I just smiled as if it was something I did every day, don't you know? Julia smiled back, but I could see understanding in her eyes, especially when there was a man suddenly lounging on the porch of the seemingly abandoned home.

"Excuse me...hey!" The man exclaimed loudly when the two of us suddenly turned and ran the other way, running up the hill and around the bend in front of the old school.

We ducked around the corner of the building, and I waited quietly. I sent Julia along at a brisk walk, almost as if she had suddenly forgotten something. If she was followed, I knew the men were up to no good. If no one showed up, we would just head on back down the hill another way.

A minute later, three men hurried past. They were about my age, but skinnier and greasier-looking. Their clothes were mismatched pick-ups, and they had various weapons, which peeked out from under their jackets and shirts. The leader, if that's what he was, was slightly taller, with a lean look that usually meant a cruel streak. The other two were as unmemorable as they were ugly. Lank hair and pudgy, they could almost pass for twins. They had the sloped shoulders of the weak, and were probably vicious to make up for it.

Julia was about fifty yards ahead when the leader called out. "Hey, pretty lady! You mind if I talk to you for a minute?"

Julia smiled prettily. "Thank you! Sure thing! What can I do for you?" Julia could play at stupid really well when she wanted to. She turned and faced the man squarely, cocking her hip and tilting her head to the side. I almost felt sorry for the man; he was being set up so well.

I slipped out of my hiding spot and moved along the ditch of the road, trying to keep a low profile. It wasn't easy, since I would almost surely be seen before I could get close enough to make a difference.

"Well, sweetie, I was hoping you might ask that." The leader leered at Julia, obviously sizing her up and liking what he saw. "You see, I'm a recruiter, and I am out here at the capital looking for pretty ladies to ask if they want to partake in a business opportunity."

Julia scowled. "Do you mean, like, a job?" She glanced my way and crossed her arms under her breasts, lifting them slightly and capturing the full attention of the pudgy brothers.

"That's right, darling. A job. My boss wants me to find really pretty ladies like you to work around the town and help out with things that need to get done." Leader was in his full pitch, thinking he had one hooked. Julia was acting as if she was really interested, and not watching the two men who were edging around her from both sides.

I was close enough that I was able to get out into the street and behind the leader. The other two men hadn't seen me, and I was just going to wait to see what would happen. Maybe these guys were legitimate with their job offer. Maybe Julia wanted another line of work. Maybe the next game the kids will try is Kiss the Zombie. Who knew?

About a second later, I did. The leader wrapped up his spiel and put his hands on his hips. I could see at least two knives from my vantage point and a third that was peeking out of his sleeve. Julia pretended to think, and then said, "Sorry, I don't think so." She started to turn and leave when the two other men stepped in her way.

"I'm afraid I do think so, darling. I think you're going to take that job, and take it right now!" The leader reached a hand towards his back pocket, where I could see a pair of handcuffs was sitting.

Before the man even finished talking, Julia was already moving. She ducked down and rolled backwards, coming up behind the two startled pudgy ones with a slim dagger in each hand. The blades were seven inches long, razor sharp, and as pointy as needles.

"Don't make this difficult, missy. I'd hate to hurt you." The leader stepped forward but stopped suddenly, his hands coming up to his neck to grasp at my hand, which had grabbed him from behind. I turned him quickly to the left, ramming my left fist into his stomach in an attempt to locate his spine. The air left him in a pained groan and he fell to the ground retching.

"Funny," I said, grinning at the two pudgy ones. "I really enjoyed hurting *him*." I dropped my hands to my sides and when I raised them again, I was holding my 'hawk and my knife. "This conversation is over." I crouched slightly, taking in both men at once. I was already planning my moves should they attack, something my dad taught me to do so much it was reflex.

The two men looked at me, and then looked at Julia, who winked at the one with the bleach highlights in his hair. The man didn't return the favor, and with a shrug, they reached down and collected their boss. Truth was, they probably would have fought, but they decided it would be better to stay in the graces of their leader than die while trying to avenging him.

As they dragged him away, one of them fired a parting shot. "We'll remember you, mister. And you, girlie. We'll get you, too."

Something went cold inside me and I suddenly bolted for the man. He threw his hands up in defense, but I used the downward slope for momentum and kicked him in the chest, knocking him dozens of feet down the hill. He came to a stop against a light pole, and I half wondered what it would take to get the attention of the law in this town. I turned on his friend, but that one skipped backwards so fast I'd have a hard time chasing him. The man on the ground must have been feeling better, so much so that, when he looked up at me with hate-filled eyes, I returned the favor with a kick to his crotch. He keeled over and grabbed his wounded jewels, making small mewing sounds through his pain.

"Come on, Julia, let's get the hell out of here. These three aren't even entertaining," I said, sheathing my weapons. Julia had already put hers away, and as we walked past the still standing fat guy, she lunged suddenly at him, causing him to lose his balance and fall into a rather large puddle.

As we left the trio, I glanced back and saw the men returning to their leader, trying to get him to stand up and having their efforts rebuked. I laughed inwardly, but I wondered what my father would have done, seeing what was happening to a town he helped to revive and save?

"Think Jake is all right?" Julia asked, looking around at the corners and alleyways as we hurried away from the last altercation.

"Likely. He doesn't attract too much attention."

"Jake?"

"Usually."

"Jake?"

"Sometimes?" I knew I was reaching, and knew that we could have a big fight on our hands if Jake went a little off the chain. Given the mood that he woke up in, and the trouble we had, I figured if Jake hadn't blown by now, he wasn't going to.

CHAPTER 12

We moved down the hill and back towards the river front area. People were moving about, going about their business and lives, and there was a general energy to the place. There was something, else, though, something that didn't have a specific name to it. I felt it when we stood down by the candle shop and hardware store.

People walking around didn't look up too much, and when they did, it was just a quick glance, here and there. They walked a little too quickly, held their purchases a little too tightly, and didn't seem to trust themselves to speak too loudly.

I noticed several of the older inhabitants would scowl from time to time, and they were more apt to speak up, but in general, something was off. I wondered if Julia noticed as well, but she was busy picking up a small ball that had bounced near her feet. A child, likely no more than five, came shyly over and stood about six feet away. He looked at her with big brown eyes, and slowly held out a hand for the ball Julia was holding.

"Peez?" He said, keeping his hand outstretched with the other tucked under his chin. I looked up and saw another small child peeking cautiously over a small fence that closed off a tiny yard. The back gate was open, and explained how the youngster managed to get out after his ball.

A voice called out from the house before Julia could hand him the ball.

"Jimmy? Jimmy! Where are you? Jimmy!"

A young mother, probably no older than Julia, came racing out of the house and scooped up the other child. She raced through the gate and spotted her other offspring. Running over, she put a protective hand on Jimmy's head and knelt down by him.

"Don't ever leave the yard! You know that!" The woman clutched both children close and I wondered what was causing this fear.

"But, Mommy, the ball..." Jimmy held out his hand again and Julia stepped over and gave him the ball.

"Sorry, miss, he was just trying to get his ball back," Julia said kindly.

The woman noticed Julia for the first time and gave her a once over. Julia's beauty sometimes put women off, but this woman was pretty enough herself not to be bothered.

"Thank you. He's all I have, and with the kidnappings lately, it's been a constant nightmare," She said, holding Jimmy, who ignored the proceedings and wandered back to the yard. The woman watched them both go back and turned to Julia. "Thanks again." She turned back to her little house when a harsh voice launched itself across the intersection.

"Hey! Where you going? Where you live, pretty thing?" A man about thirty came walking down the street, and many people got out of his way. He was about my height, but he was massive, with fat arms and a large gut. His face was covered with a coarse beard, almost looking like fur, and his deep-set eyes were mean and dark. Big hands swung without regard to hitting anyone, and people seemed to scramble to get out of the way.

The woman stopped where she was and waited her head down and arms to her sides. Instantly, I was in kill mode, and I didn't even understand why.

"Hey! Turn around when Carson Casey talks to you!" The man walked closer, and Julia turned to face him. That seemed to set him off even more. "Lookie here! We can have a threesome! Ha!' The man barked at his own joke and stepped closer. Behind him, I could see another man watching the scene with interest. He was tall, but thin, and his eyes had a calculating look about them. I committed his face to memory, because I figured I would see it again.

I was about to intervene when Jake suddenly appeared. He had a knife in his hand and a very calm look on his face. He stepped between the women and Carson, and the fat man nearly fell over trying to stop in time.

"That's far enough." Jake's voice was quiet, and from experience, I knew he was not in the mood for talking.

I stepped out and positioned myself about fifteen feet back and to the left of Carson. I didn't want to watch the proceedings. I was more interested in making sure no one came to Carson's aid. But I could see Jake from where I was. Three men detached themselves from the front of the wine shop, but stopped when I casually took out my tomahawk and tested the edge with my thumb.

"Who the fuck are you?" Casey roared at Jake. He kept his eyes on the knife Jake was holding, but he clearly didn't think Jake was any sort of threat.

"Friends call me Jake. You can call me sir, if it suits you," Jake said, holding his knife up and inspecting the blade.

"Fuck that, you little prick. Put that knife away before I shove it up your ass and make you smile while I do it." Casey started to move towards Jake, but Jake just put the blade out in front of himself, stopping Carson's forward progress.

"Have I told you what I do for a living?" Jake asked, locking eyes with Casey.

"Fuck do I care? Step the fuck aside!" Clearly, Carson was limited in his vocabulary choices.

"I'm a Collector, Casey," Jake said, staring intently at his blade.

Casey's manner changed abruptly. When he first thought he was up against some fool who wanted to defend some poor girls honor due to some misguided feelings of chivalry, he figured to just brush the fool aside and be done with it. When that fool turned out to be someone who confronted zombie hordes on a regular basis and lived to tell the tale, then that was something else entirely.

Casey still tried to bull his way through. "I'm done talking. Move or I'll break your fucking..."

Whatever Carson meant to say was lost as Jake struck suddenly, stepping up close to Casey and pressing the blade of his knife against the larger man's throat. Jake then moved his face close to Casey and said something that scared the man to his roots.

"I've killed zombies with this blade two days ago, Carson, and I don't remember if I cleaned it properly." Jake smiled slightly, almost apologetically.

Carson Casey suddenly broke out in a sweat. Everyone over the age of fifteen knew the threat of zombies, and everyone else knew what to do to keep from getting infected and turning themselves. Jake's dirty blade was a death sentence and Casey knew it. One cut and it was over. Nothing could save the big man from becoming a zombie except a crack in the skull.

"D-Don't do anything stupid, son, I was j-just funnin' with the ladies," Casey said shakily.

"I'm sure you were. But they might have not liked your manner, so I'm sure you will apologize, correct?" Jake tended to get precise when he was in a bad mood, but Casey would never know how close to death he really was.

Carson's eyes narrowed but he managed to creak out a sincere-sounding apology. I might have felt sorry for the man if he hadn't been such a prick earlier.

"Excellent," Jake said. "Now we can all be friends again." He pulled the knife away from the big man's throat and Carson fairly fell back in an attempt to get away from the poisoned blade. I looked at my tomahawk and then looked back at the men lounging nearby and they suddenly realized they had other places to be.

Carson stalked away and Jake came over to where I was standing.

"Think this might be trouble later?" he asked.

I knew what he was saying, and I didn't feel like getting into trouble, so I lied.

"Should be alright. If we were staying it would be, but I don't think so." I knew Jake would finish the man off if he felt he had a reason, and I didn't want to stay any longer.

"Hope so." Jake turned to the young woman who had never left Julia's side. As he approached, I saw Julia sheath a knife at the small of her back. Carson Casey would have died one way or the other today.

"Sorry for the trouble, ma'am." Jake said to the young mother. "Hope that fool doesn't bother you anymore."

The woman blushed. "He's been a pain, but I can't fight him with my babies nearby."

"If you need help, just have someone get in touch with us. We'll take care of things," Jake promised.

"Thank you." She turned to Julia. "Thank you." After that, she went back to her little yard where her children were quietly playing with the ball again.

We stood together in the street. I noticed a lot of people smiled at us, and several nodded in approval. I had the feeling Casey was not well liked, and I wondered if it might have been a kindness to the town to have run him out. The man lounging had disappeared, but I still had the feeling I was going to see him again.

Jake tilted his head towards the docks, and when we had cleared the last of the shops, he showed us the three gold coins and two silver coins he had managed to get out of the Melter for his jewelry. Julia laughed and brought out the payment from Charlie, and we all looked at the new wealth we had managed to accumulate within a very short amount of time.

"Dang," Jake said, looking over the money. "Anything we need before we shove off and head for home? Anything? House, car, boat?"

We all laughed, but the reality was we had enough money for a car or a boat. After the world came to an end, the new Congress decided to use precious metals for currency. They established the rate of exchange and made sure everyone followed by example. The money was copper, silver, and gold. All paper money was completely worthless. Our dads had insisted, saying this was one lesson from the past we were going to learn. Twenty copper coins equaled a silver coin, and twenty silvers equaled a gold coin. Once it was announced that we were going back to a gold standard, there was a rush to procure old jewelry, watches, and rings. After the initial rush died down, people let the marketplace dictate prices, and they were off.

It worked out well, since there was no arguing that there was plenty to go around. Jewelry stores that had survived the zombies were suddenly very popular and most within the vicinity of any town were looted, and quickly.

We pocketed our wealth and made our way back to our boat. We expected the trip to be very uneventful, but it wasn't going to start out that way. Standing by our docked canoe was a large man flanked by two others. All three were armed with firearms, something unusual in the settled areas. There wasn't any law against them, people just left them behind, most of the time.

I expected serious trouble and was calculating how I could throw my hawk faster than any of the men could draw their weapons when the man in front spoke.

"Are you three leaving Leport?" He wasn't much for conversation, and I felt an immediate bond with the man.

"Who wants to know?" Jake asked, looking the men over.

"Name's Lane Tucker. I'm the law." The answer was short and to the point. I liked that, and my instincts were telling me good things about this guy.

"Have we done something wrong?" Jake asked, more polite this time. Dad had always brought us up to respect the law. You didn't have to respect the man representing it, but you had to respect the law itself.

"No, I just wanted to thank you for dealing with that bully Casey. He's always pushing the boundaries, but never fully crosses them." Lane looked over our shoulders at the town. "Yet," he added.

"Tucker, we don't want trouble, but twice today we've had run ins when before we would have to go looking for trouble ourselves. What's going on around here?" I asked.

Lane threw me a look that was part approval, and part admiration. "You've hit on something. There's something going on, and we can't quite get a handle on it. People have gone missing, a new element is in town, and most it is all bad. I feel like half the time I'm chasing ghosts." He looked out over the river. "Sometimes I wish the zombies would come back. At least then people would have an enemy with a face, not just something hidden under the surface."

Jake surprised me with his next statement. "Tough luck, Tucker. But if you need any help, give us a call. We'll back you if you need it."

I was stunned. Jake was usually more than ready to let people solve their own problems. But here he was, volunteering us for something that really wasn't any of our business.

Lane Tucker held out his hand. "I may do that, son. I just may do that." He motioned to his men and the three started back towards the town.

"Tucker!" Jake called.

Lane turned back. "What is it?"

"Should I have killed Casey?"

Lane thought about it for a moment. "Yes," he said as he walked away.

Jake nodded and we got back into our canoe, pushing off and heading down the canal towards home.

CHAPTER 13

We were quiet for a long time, passing under the bridges that led to the other side of the river.

Finally Jake spoke. "If I don't see the capital again for a while, I won't be too sorry."

"I would agree with that," I said, angling the canoe to hit the swifter currents of the shallows.

Julia spent the next few minutes relating to Jake what had transpired after the delivery of the goods. Jake listened quietly, and looked back once to nod after hearing my part in it.

"Place needs some changing. Don't know what, though, outside of a good fire." Jake paddled a bit more, speeding us towards the spillway and the generating station.

"Yup." I matched his strokes and together we moved towards home. We wouldn't get there until morning, home being over sixty five miles by water away, but we'd make good time and spend the night at one of our stopping places. It didn't matter too much where we were, no one was waiting for us at home anyway.

We paddled and drifted until the sun began its descent, and we found ourselves at Goose Lake Prairie Preserve. I moved us across Heidecke Lake and headed for the docks.

"Good call, Aaron," Jake called out. "My arms were getting tired."

"Me, too," Julia said.

"What?" I yelped. "You haven't done anything but keep our packs warm and stick your fingers in the water!" I directed this at Julia.

"Someone had to do it. It's a tough job." Julia tried to say this with a straight face, but failed miserably.

I slapped the water with my paddle and managed to slice a bit of water over the side of the canoe. My aim was of and I hit Jake in the head.

"Hey!" Jake yelled while Julia giggled.

"Sorry!" I called, trying to correct the boat as it started to swing in the current. The docks were actually behind a couple of breakers, and getting into the harbor without a motor was tricky.

Jake growled and slapped the water with his own paddle, sending a decent wave up and behind him.

It would have been very effective had Julia not been in the way. As it was, she took the brunt of the wave in her face, leaving her sputtering and cursing. I laughed, and she would have gone for water to hit me with if I hadn't threatened to tip the damn canoe over and drown the both of them.

We slipped into the harbor laughing, and it was good to get the tension out of ourselves. Leport had left a bad taste in our mouths, and we needed to release it somehow.

Docking the canoe, we tied it off and walked over to the grassy area which used to be a picnic area, by the looks of things. The grass was about knee high, but we could still see the old tables, and the pavilion was still standing, although the roof was starting to slew to one side.

I walked around in a small area, checking for rocks, before I put up my little one-man tent. Jake and Julia did the same, and as the sun started to set, we talked about the trip and about what we were going to do next.

"Ever think about doing something else?" Jake asked.

"Like what?" I replied. "We weren't raised for much else."

"Maybe," Jake said. "Maybe we *were* raised for something else, we just haven't figured out what it is."

I looked at Jake as if he was nuts. "We were brought up to be able to do one thing: survive. We trained to fight both zombies and men, and all of our skills have brought us one source of income: going where no one else wants to go." I stood up and looked out over the river. "Face it, Jake, it's all we were supposed to do."

"Not good enough, little brother. I keep thinking there's a purpose behind this, behind everything that's happened. I can't explain it, but I'm trying to figure out what it is." Jake seemed as if he was about to say something else, but he stopped himself.

"What does your gut say, Jake?" Julia asked, interrupting the silence.

Jake looked at her. "It says we were meant to do more than just be garbage collectors." Over our protests, he said loudly, "Let's be real. We go and risk our necks for crap that other people haven't got the guts to go get. When does it end? When do we reach the point where everything anyone has ever wanted is going to be collected?" Jake looked out over the water to the West. "I just have been feeling lately that there's something more we're supposed to be doing."

"Well, big brother, when you figure it out, you let me know. For now, we're collectors," I said, stretching out and watching the stars slowly blink into existence in the purpling sky.

"Something to think about, Aaron," Jake said.

"Now what?"

"Why are we saving our money? What's the point?"

"What do you mean?" I had to admit I hadn't been expecting this line from Jake.

"We've got a lot of money from our collecting. Why? We don't need food or shelter. We're able to go into the grey zones and get whatever we need. Why the money? What's our end game with it?" Jake sounded like he had been giving this a lot more than just a cursory thought or two.

"Go to sleep."

"Just wondering, little brother."

I closed my eyes, but Jake's words had struck a chord. What *were* we getting paid for?

CHAPTER 14

We packed up early in the morning and got underway while the river and the surrounding countryside were still asleep. The sun hadn't come up yet, but the grey dawn was turning blue and the sun was very close behind.

We passed Ottawa and Morris, and there was a bit of urgency in our strokes as we got closer to home. Julia was more anxious than normal, and we would be happy to walk familiar paths once again.

Around mid-morning, we pulled into the dock. Our big motorboats looked at us in askance, wondering when we would take them out for a stretch. Across the river, at Eagle Island, the livestock wandered to the river's edge for their morning drink. I looked up towards Eagle Point, but as usual, no one was there. It would have been nice to see a couple of tall figures standing there, but as I had come to expect, that probably wasn't going to happen.

After tying up our canoe, we walked in silence up the hill and across the lawn. It hadn't been cut in several days, and was starting to get a little fuzzy. I could see Jake scowling at it and I knew he would be out cutting it as soon as he could. I never figured out why Jake did that, it was something he picked up a couple of years ago. I guess it kept him busy.

We passed the guesthouse, which once upon a time was the Visitor Center to the park we lived in. I don't know why we had a guest house, since we lived in a lodge that had hundreds of rooms, but we needed it for something.

Climbing up the stairs, we went from forest floor to forest canopy. The landscape spread out before us, and as always, I was struck by the beauty and solitude of the place we called home. The river, the forest, the rock formations, the canyons, and the trails, all made this a fantastic place to live. The only thing missing was differentiated company, but we got enough of that on our travels to the various towns and cities.

Once inside, we dropped our gear in the storeroom and went our separate ways. The first thing on my list was a shower, and I didn't doubt it was first on the list for Julia and

Jake. I went up to my suite of rooms, noting the still closed door across the hall. One of these days, Jake and I will open it, but it still hurt a lot.

An hour later, I was in the main lounge area by the fireplace, burning off any excess zombie glop from my weapons and sharpening their already razor-sharp edges. My sword took the longest, mostly because it was over thirty inches of cutting edge.

Julia came in, rubbing her hair with a towel and wearing clean clothes.

"You busy?" She asked.

"Not really," I said, running an oily rag over my blade and sheathing it. "What's up?"

"Nothing, I was just going to go visit mom, and wanted to know if you wanted to come with."

I thought for a second. "Yeah, maybe that might be what I need."

"Come on." Julia took my hand and together we headed out of the lodge and down the stairwell. We crossed the main area, and I smiled when I saw Jake working the lawn mower, clearing out the tall grass, and keeping the place looking like it always had, even back in the day when the place was a spot for tourists. Never could figure out why he did that, and he wasn't telling.

We climbed the main steps of the chimney rock formation that rose out of the riverside and stood like a sentinel over the Illinois River. At the top, we looked out for a moment at the big bend in the river, easily being able to discern the town of Ottawa. Over to the west and north, Utica could be seen, although there wasn't much left. The years had not been kind, and two out of every three buildings were caved in and covered in brush. In the river was a small dam, and through it, a small generating station provided us with power.

Julia tugged at my hand.

"Come on. We didn't come up here to see the sights."

I allowed myself to be led, and each step brought back a lot of memories and a lot of feelings. We followed a small trail to the center of the pillar, crossing ancient stones put there by the

French Army a long time ago. There had been a fort once on top of this rock, and a hotel, if the information from the Visitor Center was to be believed. But the top of this rock served another purpose, now.

We stepped into the small clearing and approached the two graves that had been dug there. Simple wooden crosses marked the gravesites, and Julia approached the one on the right. The marker simply said *Rebecca*. I went and stood by the marker on the left. This one simply said, *Sarah*.

The graves were about fifteen feet apart, and allowed for Julia and me to have some private time with our respective mothers.

"Hi, Mom," I said, sitting down on the warm grass. "I'm back."

We spent the better part of an hour, just sitting quietly and talking softly to our mothers. Julia occasionally ran her hands through the grass on the grave, sometimes holding the grass, as if she was holding her mother's hand again.

I talked of the things we had done, and mentioned how Jake was acting funny. I didn't talk about my father at all, that was a subject I tended to avoid when he wasn't here with me. It was awkward, anyway.

As the sun went higher, Julia finally kissed her hand and placed it on the name on the marker. That was her signal it was time for goodbyes, and I said my own, standing quickly. It had been two years since our mothers had passed away. Two years since our fathers silently dug these graves. Two years since we had last seen our fathers. One morning we woke up to find our dads' weapons gone, their truck missing, and a note on the table that just said:

This place isn't home right now.
We have things to do.
Don't follow.

Jake went a little nuts for a while, being angry all the time and blaming our dads for all the ills of the world. However, as the days passed and the hurts started to heal, Jake began to get over it. He seemed his normal self for a while, but for the past month, he had been acting a little funny, and our conversation last night proved he had something in his head.

We didn't speak all the way back to the main stairwell. We just held hands, and that was nice enough for me. At the top of the stairs, we saw Jake waiting for us on the patio. He had a slip of paper in his hand and I knew what it was before he even spoke.

"Got a call from Ottawa. We got another job," Jake said, handing me the paper. It had an address on it, and the item we were going after was another heirloom.

"Where the hell is Peotone?" I asked, looking at the address and item list.

Julia looked at the items and whistled. "Looks like we might have to do some heavy hauling for this one."

She wasn't kidding . The items included a set of books, a .22 rifle, and a roll-top desk.

"A desk? Seriously? I hope you said no," I said, shaking my head in disbelief. We'd had strange requests before, and there were some things we said no to as a matter of logistics. We had gone after cameras, sweaters, and the occasional chair or two, but a desk? What was next, a piano?

"I didn't say yes, but I said we'd try our best," Jake said with a smile. "We can take the truck, it shouldn't be a problem."

"Why can't we take a boat?" I had no idea where Peotone was, so I assumed it was accessible by boat like most of our outings.

Julia fielded that one. "Peotone is in the middle of literally nowhere, surrounded on all sides by fields. In normal farm country it's be a cakewalk."

"Let me guess. It isn't normal farm country," I said bleakly.

"Big prize for the big boy," Jake said. "It's right smack dab in the middle of a grey corridor, being one of the towns that connects directly to the interstate." A grey corridor was a section of the country that ran alongside a highway. You could live in it, but the threat of zombies was increased because of its proximity to a highway that once had transported thousands of fleeing people, and thousands of infected people. A lot of the towns were just abandoned, and it looked like Peotone was one of them.

"Which one?" It didn't matter, but by this time, I figured I would at least sound interested.

"I-57," Jake said, "Right off the main connection to the city itself."

"Great." I couldn't have been more sarcastic if I took lessons. Ordinarily I would be fine, but we just got back from zombie central, not to mention a couple of altercations in the capital that left a bad taste in my mouth. Add it all up and I had a serious case of the 'no wannas.'

"What's the pay?" Julia asked.

"I decided to up the rate, since this was a big item. If we managed to get the desk, we would require an additional two gold pieces and five silvers. Not that we'd have anything we were saving the money for, right?" Jake cocked a side grin at me and I came close to knocking him on the head for it.

"All right. When do you want to go?" I figured it was better to stay busy than bored and get to thinking about all of the things that weren't quite right with my world.

Jake mused for a minute, taking the time to look out over the treetops. "Let's take a day to get our bearings back, then another to set up and plan, and take off on the third. Cool?"

I was good with it, but Julia apparently wasn't.

"Hey, guys. I think I want to sit this one out." Julia seemed nervous; as if she was fearful, we would make fun of her.

Jake cocked his head and gave her the full brunt of his brown eyes. "What's up? You got a boyfriend somewhere?"

Julia snorted. "With you two around? Who could compete? No, I just want to get some things done around here that need doing; that have needed doing for a long time."

Jake nodded, and I think he might have actually understood more than Julia was giving him credit for. I knew for sure when he spoke again.

"You're right. I think Jake and I may be doing the same, maybe on this trip," Jake said.

It was my turn to look confused. "What?"

Jake laughed. "All in good time, Aaron, all in good time. Let's get some lunch."

CHAPTER 15

The day off flew by, and by the time the second day was here, my head was already on the trip. Jake and I sat at the big table in the lounge area and mapped out the route. Essentially, we were going to be heading south and then west, with very little activity in between. That was okay with me. The last trip had been a little tense, so I could handle easy this time around.

"The biggest thing we need to worry about is fuel. We can fill up in Ottawa, then that will get us as far as Peotone, which seems to be about eighty miles, one way, and back. We'll be tight, but we can do it. I just hope the desk doesn't cause serious problems," Jake said.

"If it does, we ditch it and don't take payment for it. Simple." I looked at the map and pointed. "Can we take highways?"

"We can take I-80 for the trip over to the west, but I don't know the condition of I-57. If it's bad, we'll have to take another route." Jake seemed anxious to get going, but I didn't want to move until tomorrow.

"All right. Are we packed yet?" I asked.

"Not yet. If we're done here, let's get to it."

"I'll get the truck."

I went outside to the garage, and pulled out the truck we used for off-river collections. It was a Ford F-150 king cab, with a lift kit that raised the vehicle an additional ten inches. Big tires allowed for off-road capability, and this bad boy was fully four-wheel drive. The only downside was a slew of flower stickers that Julia had stuck on the back window when she was a little girl, and we never got around to taking them off. It wasn't easy trying to be tactical when your ride had flowers on it.

I piled my pack behind the seat and put my rifle in a storage rack as well. I was partial to the heavy hitting M1A, while Jake preferred the simplicity of the SIG 556. It's piston-recoil mechanism was easy to maintain, and my military weapon was easy as well. We didn't use our heavy guns all that much, but we never left them behind.

After packing the truck, Jake and I sparred for a bit, keeping ourselves loose and trained. Jake was a little more deliberate this time, and though he tagged me couple of times, I rang his bell enough to get his attention. Julia came in to watch our last session, and she studied our moves, looking for weaknesses for the time when she challenged one of us to fight.

Jake and I squared off one last time, and this time I waited for him to come to me. He didn't disappoint. Jake darted forward, ducking down and striking out with his left foot, hoping to get me to step back so he could straighten up and swing a kick with his right. I decided to force the issue sooner so I crouched down, bringing up my right leg and punching for his gut with my left hand. I connected with his shoulder and forced him back, straightening him up and getting him to stumble a bit.

I pressed forward and kicked out with my right foot, landing a solid kick on his thigh, knocking him onto his back. I stood up and stepped forward, catching Jake as he slammed a shoulder into my gut. He had rolled backwards, and then launched himself as soon as his feet were under him. I could feel his arms wrap around me, but if I stayed standing, the advantage would be mine.

I swung a leg back, stopping my backward movement. Jake grabbed my knee, but I brought it up faster and connected with his gut. I slammed down with my elbow, knocking his breath out, then grabbed him around the waist and spun to the right, lifting him off his feet and tossing him into the wall. He landed hand, and then bounced to his feet, his face a mask of rage and his eyes flinty.

"All right, then. Baby brother wants to play," Jake said , moving forward and bringing his hands up.

I knew I was in for it, but I was strangely calm. I had never bested Jake so easily, and with an ego like his, it had to be difficult to swallow, especially with Julia watching.

Jake feinted with his left and hit me with his right, although I just managed to block the second punch. Jake then launched a series of attacks that rained blows on my arms and head, although I managed to avoid the worst of them. A punch got through my defenses and hit me square in the gut. As I went over, I threw an uppercut to try and get Jake to back off, not realizing he was coming in to try and finish me off.

The punch landed on Jake's chin and snapped his head back, causing him to drop his arms and fall to the ground in a heap. As I recovered, I noticed Jake wasn't moving, and Julia was coming over to check on him.

As she rolled him over, I could hear Jake say, "Check his hands for bricks, would you, please?" I guessed Jake would be okay.

We waited a day longer than we had planned, mostly because Jake didn't want to go out in public with a big lump on his chin. I didn't do much to help, I kept giggling every time I saw him, and Julia was no help either. She kept leaving bricks where Jake could find them, and to his credit, Jake said nothing.

On the night, before we were to leave, though, Julia woke the local dead screaming about the load of bricks Jake had piled in her bed. I just closed my door and let the two of them fight it out.

CHAPTER 16

In the morning, Jake and I climbed into the truck and headed out, waving to Julia as we left. We knew she would be all right by herself. No one in their right mind would try to attack the park, as a family of cougars roamed in the woods and kept it free from trespassers. Not to mention, Julia was a crack shot and deadly with her weapons. No worries there.

Jake drove, and we headed out along Route 71. That road took us on a southerly tour of the edge of our domain, and into the river lands. The road twisted a lot at the eastern edge of the preserve, and since we were really bad about maintaining the roads, it took us an hour to navigate the turns and hills. When we cleared the hills, it was straight sailing to Ottawa, the big city on the river. Once upon a time, zombies had overrun this town, but after a serious pushback by our dad, people had been coming back. There had to be over five thousand people there now, and seemed to be growing daily.

We filled up at the one gas station in town, paying a silver for our gas and getting a handful of coppers in change. Gas was extremely cheap, something my dad explained as the law of supply and demand, but I never paid attention when he started going on about economics.

A small jog north took us to the interstate, and we were able to make pretty good time. The irony was the main highway swung north, and would have actually put us in Peotone's backyard had it stayed straight. As it was, we were travelling an extra twenty miles out of our way, but it was faster and easier travelling, so it was okay.

All other roads were maintained as well as could be expected, but the highway was a priority. We had to be able to respond to an emergency in case of another outbreak, so the main highways had been cleared from the Appalachians to the Rockies. It had taken ten years, and even Jake and I worked on it, but it was necessary.

An hour into the ride, Jake took us over the bridge at Joslin. That town had never recovered from the big outbreak, and it was still a ghost town. Teenagers dared each other to go into the dark buildings at night, and everyone in a while little pinpoints of light could be seen walking around at dusk. There were places in Joslin that even the best of collectors refused to go, and the whole place had been declared off limits by the government several years ago.

"Bet there's some neat stuff down there," Jake said, riding over the bridge. The big tires made a humming sound as we passed it.

"Want to go look?" I figured Jake was bluffing so I decided to call him on it.

"No, thanks. I promised Dad I would look out for you. Can't do that when I put you in the vicinity of thousands of ghouls.

I looked over at Jake. "When did you promise him anything? All you ever did was argue with him, fight over any training he wanted you to have, and bitch about him leaving."

Jake looked at me for a long moment, and I held his gaze. I was starting to realize why our father left, and in part, understand it.

"You wouldn't understand. You never understand," Jake said, turning back to the road. I knew by that tone the conversation had ended.

We rode in silence until we reached the junction of I-80 and I-57. The 80 side was fine, but the 57 side was a mess. There were literally thousands of rusting cars jammed all over the road, and a single lane had been cleared for people to drive on. And by cleared I mean a large fork truck had come through, lifted the cars out of the way, and dumped them in the next lane. It was a weird sight, seeing cars just stacked on top of each other, flattened in some places, rusted together in others. Many of the cars had skeletons still in them, and there were even a few that sported still moving zombies. They were in awful shape, but the closed environments kept them protected from the sun and cold. If they ever managed to get out, they would be as dangerous as ever.

The bad part of this trip was the piled cars were on my side, so I had nothing to look at except mile after mile of rusted cars and dead flesh. I only got a glimpse of the countryside when there was a brief space here and there where the cars were not piled on each other.

The exits were blocked by gate secured by concrete pylons, but you could get out and open the gate, as long as you closed it behind yourself. The idea was to keep as many of the zombies that were still on the roads contained as much as possible. Occasionally one would slip through, but they were dealt with quickly.

"Zombie, dead ahead," Jake said, chuckling at his own joke.

I groaned. We'd used that one to death, but it still drew a chuckle from time to time. "All right. I'll deal with it," I said. Jake pulled up about twenty yards from the zombie and stopped the truck. I climbed out, grateful for the chance to stretch my legs. The zombie was slowly walking towards us, and it was just about the most awful zombie I had seen. The flesh had been ripped from its torso and legs, hanging down in massive strips. Its clothes were mostly gone, being torn down one side, and missing from the other. Its head was fairly intact, in fact the flesh was only slightly ripped. This one used to be a female, and her one good eye stared at me intently as she stumbled forward. It was particularly gross to see her step on her own strips of skin, tearing even more of it off.

"Ugh," was all I had to say. I went over to a rusty car and nodded at the zombie still trapped inside. It raised a hand to gently touch the window, then watched me as I kicked and twisted its front bumper off. If it hadn't been so rusted, I could never had done that.

Turning back to the skinless zombie, I took the bumper and shoved the jagged end straight into her forehead. The sharp metal broke through her skull and killed her instantly. I pulled out the bumper and reversed it, using the slightly hooked end to grab her under her chin and drag her out of the way. I left the bumper with her and climbed back into the truck.

"Nice one," Jake said.

"Thanks."

"I think that one wins the prize for most disgusting."

"For sure. You know how it got that way?" The solution seemed obvious once I thought of it.

"Do tell."

"Twisting and pulling out of a seat belt." I was fairly impressed with myself.

Jake thought for a minute as we pulled past the ex-zombie. "That makes sense. Nasty way to end up. Wonder what prompted her to free herself?"

"Probably someone like us taking a trip, only maybe they were walking instead of riding."

"Could be. Could be." Jake steered through the cars, following the path put before him by someone who wished for a southern route away from everything. Truth be told, it was probably faster to take the back roads, but this was a mostly direct route, and it would also provide us with a path back, provided the other side was clear as well.

After an hour of this kind of travel, Jake decided he'd had enough, and we'd head towards Peotone via a more indirect route.

We pulled up to the gate at the exit for Route 30, and I jumped out again, untying the rope that held the gate shut, and pulling the gate aside. Jake slipped the truck past, and I closed and retied the gate, keeping zombies like our friend the stripper from getting out and causing outbreaks.

This part of Route 30 took us through Matteson, and it wasn't very pretty. A big hotel stood off to the side, and the tall atrium windows would have looked nice if they hadn't been blown out from the inside by a fire that had claimed the building years before. Several other buildings were in similar states, and those that survived the first wave of zombies fell to the second wave of looters. Mother Nature took it from there, tearing up the parking lots and dumping rain and mold all over the place. A couple of places had fallen so far into nature that they looked like misshapen hills.

CHAPTER 17

As we drove through the businesses, it was hard to imagine this place had once been a thriving community. However, neglect, years of hammering by nature, and looting had taken its final toll. In another twenty years, places that hadn't been reclaimed were going to disappear.

"Company," Jake said suddenly, looking ahead at the road. We had turned down Route 50 and were headed south.

"Friendly?" I asked, looking to see for myself. I wouldn't be put out if I couldn't see them yet. Jake had eyes like a hawk's, and could easily make out details of something most people could barely see.

"Not sure. They just appeared over that small road that crosses the railroad tracks."

"Time to arm?" I started to reach back for my M1A when Jake stopped me.

"Hang on. Let's get a little closer and see what they do. Let's make ourselves a little bit more tempting," Jake said.

"How?" I asked. Do you want me to dress like a female and blow them kisses as we go past?"

"Not quite. Get down, below the dash, so they can't see you. If they're friendly, they'll wish me the best and let me go. If they think we're easy pickings, they'll follow and look for a way to get me out of my vehicle or they'll come up alongside and shoot me with something loud."

I had to admit it made sense in a weird kind of way. I guess that comes from always looking at the pessimistic side of things.

I ducked down and kept a low profile, easing my M1A out from behind the seat. That was tricky but doable. I put the muzzle just out of sight under the window and waited. Jake opened the back window and drove on, seemingly blissful in his ignorance of human intentions.

I had no way of knowing what was happening outside, but Jake kept me up to date.

"Okay, we're passing them now. Hey guys!" Jake threw a wave at them, partly to check their intentions and partly to keep their attention focused on him and not on what might be in the cab of the truck, namely me.

"Nothing so far, looks to be two of them in a decent-sized truck. Staying on the side road. Whoops, here they come." Jake kept an eye on the road and an eye on his mirrors.

"Coming up behind right now, staying close. Think they're checking things out, seeing if it's worth the trouble. Their rig is as nice as ours, can't see why they'd want to hijack this one." Jake looked into the rear-view and raised his head, acknowledging the truck behind him.

"Staying back there. Passenger is doing something, wait a second. He's waving me to pull over. Yeah, like that's going to happen." Jake smiled big and waved back, acting as if he was just too dumb to understand sign language.

"Okay, they're talking to each other. Passenger is reaching for something. Oh, boy. He just waved a big gun at me and wants me to pull over." Jake looked down at me. "They're directly behind me. Go for it."

I popped up suddenly, sticking the barrel of the rifle out the back window, aiming directly at the windshield of the truck behind us. I could see the passenger holding up what looked like a revolver, but my aim was more to the center. I fired once, and the heavy bullet punched through the windshield, leaving a large hole and several cracks behind. The rear window didn't fare so well, completely shattering and falling into the bed of the truck.

The two men, boys really, now that I got a look at them, got huge in the eyes and their mouths dropped open. I could see both of them shouting "*Jesus!*" and the truck suddenly slewed to the left, slamming the passenger into the side window as the pickup careened away. The driver must have stomped on the gas, because the truck raced up the railroad incline, launched itself several feet in the air, and came down in a cloud of dust on the other side of the tracks. Even at our distance, I could hear crashes and clangs as the truck tried to extract itself from the railroad.

I settled back into the seat, the M1A resting between my legs. Jake looked at me and I looked back at him. We both burst out laughing, and it got so bad that Jake had to pull over and we just held our sides and laughed ourselves silly.

"Oh, my God! Did you see that guy's face plastered to the side window?" Jake laughed.

I redoubled my laughter. "Not as good as the two faces when I aimed at them. Never saw eyes so big!"

We laughed for another five minutes, and then began to settle down. Jake looked back and wondered out loud. "Wonder if they managed to get those tracks out of their butts."

"Let them be. They deserve a little discomfort, and maybe next time they'll think twice before trying to rob someone else," I said, putting my rifle back.

"If they don't , they're the slowest learners around," Jake said, checking the rear view again.

"Let's get going. I'd like to be in Peotone before evening comes," I said.

"Me, too."

We drove south on Illinois 50, and slowly made our way through the small town of Monee. Monee looked like it had been a one light town even back in the day, and it hadn't improved much in the last twenty five years. The main road had a couple of businesses on it, and the railroad tracks cut through the center of town, albeit in a trench thirty feet deep.

On the west side of town, the interstate connected to it, and we could see two hotels, a huge truck stop, and a few restaurants. Everything was collapsing and rusting, with dozens of abandoned cars and trucks.

Jake turned towards the truck stop, and I held up a hand.

"Whoa! What are you doing? This isn't the way to Peotone," I protested.

"Just want to have a look around," Jake said. "Relax. Peotone's just five miles south. Besides, maybe there's something we can use at the truck stop."

"I'm thinking it's a bad idea," I said, believing it completely. "We've had pretty good luck so far, why push it?"

Jake just smiled, and I knew I was not going to win this fight. I'd have had a better chance if I was driving, but since I wasn't, I'd just have to go along until Jake got his fill of whatever he was looking for, or I managed to get the keys off of him.

CHAPTER 18

We drove past a trucking company, and there were dozens of empty trailers all over the place. A semi had run into the side of a dozen or so parked ones, and had literally cut several in half before coming to a stop in the middle of three of them. A skeletal head hung out of the driver's window, its empty sockets staring at the cloudless sky.

The next block had a bunch of houses, but they had all been broken into, some with doors completely ripped off the hinges, others with broken windows. Several of the homes had trees and shrubs growing out of the center of them, and here and there, we could see furtive movement, as if animals darted about.

On the other side of the street was a strip mall and an auction house, but both had been burned long ago. Blackened beams and studs reached up like charred fingers, a final plea to a God that had turned His back on the world.

Past the two restaurants, which dad used to call 'fast-food places', we reached the truck stop. The place was a disaster. It was literally two hundred feet from the highway, and that proximity had killed it. There was a line of crashed and rusting cars stretching from the gas station to the highway, and several cars had smashed into each other, jamming up the works and damning those who were trapped. Dad used to say it was the strangest part of the whole ordeal. People would stay with their cars, when safety was just a few hundred feet away. All they had to do was abandon their cars. For some, that was just too much.

We got out of the truck and slowly made our way across the sea of cars and bones. A couple of cars had zombies in them, and they slowly watched us walk past. Jake wandered over to one of them, and using his mace, smashed in the window. When the zombie leaned out, Jake cracked it in the head, killing it.

"That was effective," Jake said, looking around for another one. When he didn't see one nearby, he gave it up and headed back towards the truck stop building. I followed at a distance, checking the area, making sure we weren't being followed. I don't know why, but my alarms were going off, and I didn't see anything to warrant it. That was when things usually got pretty bad.

Jake ducked under the collapsed awning of the gas islands and re-emerged a second later.

"This way is blocked," He said tightly.

"Car?"

"Bodies." Jake moved away and went around to the side of the building. I was tempted to go take a look, but considering Jake was disturbed by what he saw, then I really didn't want to look. Two things affected Jake that way. One was the bodies of little children, and the other was anything that indicated a child might have suffered. I could ask Jake why these things bothered him, but the truth be known, he didn't know himself. It was just the way it was.

We rounded the corner and made our way to the next doorway. This one had 'SHOWERS' written on it in faded letters, and when Jake opened the door, he quickly stepped aside to let anything in there that wanted out to get out without finding him in the way. The little courtesies mattered these days. It also kept you from getting a face full of bats or bugs.

Jake pulled out his flashlight and gave it a shake. The light came on after a bit, and he looked around before stepping inside. I took out my own light and followed. The interior of the truck stop was musty and damp, with a unique black mold coming out of the restroom area. Jake was careful not to disturb it, and I did the same. You learned as a kid not to touch the stuff, since you would be hacking your lungs out for a day if you breathed any of it in. One of our friends actually died from it. He coughed black crap for days before finally choking to death.

The interior was nothing but piles and piles of junk. Cowboy hats and belt buckles were scattered about, and NASCAR toys were in abundance. Anything that might have been useful was long gone, but Jake did manage to find a set of ruby-eyed skull valve caps for our tires. That in itself almost made the trip worthwhile.

I hunted around the tools section, and came up with a torque wrench and an Allen wrench set. We could sell this stuff at a nearby town, since tools were always in demand.

"Oh, my," Jake said. I looked over at him and whistled. Under a display case, Jake had found a full carton of Marlboro cigarettes. We had seen them only briefly in our lives, but we knew what they were. Cigarettes manufactured before the zombies rising became scarcer and scarcer. As the years went by, some communities had even used them as currency before the move to precious metals. What Jake was holding was easily worth a gold piece a pack, if not more.

"That was luck," I said, hoping I could find something to compare. I didn't have much hope, but you never knew.

"No kidding. We could forget this whole trip, head back now and be done with the job, just tell them that the house burned to the ground or something," Jake said, casting a sidelong look at me.

"Tempting, but we can't. You know that," I said.

Jake sighed. "Yeah, I know. 'Your word and your honor are the two things that separate you from the savages. Keep them well and you will walk among men.' I get it."

That phrase had been drilled into our heads from an early age. Dad believed it with all his heart, and it kept us from going back to the beasts we once were.

We poked around a little more, but found little of any value. There were some light kits, but no one needed those. Under a pile of toiletries, I found a box labeled 'Trojans'. I held them up to Jake.

"Any thoughts as to what these are for?" I asked.

Jake shrugged. "Anything named after a dead civilization can't be healthy for you."

I tossed it and we made our way to the back door, Jake holding his prize like it was his baby. I felt a little putout, since Jake had the big score, but the trip was still young, and I might get to even things up later.

We skirted the mold again and Jake went out the back door first. I followed and immediately bumped into Jake's back.

"What the...? Oh." The parking lot, which had been empty when we entered the truck stop, had suddenly sprouted about a dozen zombies of various shapes and sizes.

CHAPTER 19

"Got your sword?" Jake asked, putting down the cigarettes and gripping his mace with both hands.

"Back at the truck," I said, pulling out my knife and tomahawk.

"Good place for it."

"You're the one who had to come over here for a look-see."

"Blaming is not productive."

I snickered. "Especially when you're to blame, hey?"

"You're learning." Jake tensed, and I knew he was about to move. "On the left."

I looked and saw a little zombie moving fast. I hated the little things. They nearly killed us years ago and had actually managed to kill my uncle. They were fast, for whatever reason, and they were nasty. These little bastards caused ninety percent of outbreaks. The virus that caused the zombies effected kids differently. They were faster, smarter, and much more difficult to kill. Sometimes they even stalked you, which was unnerving. Once Jake actually had to chase one and kill it, which took a lot out of him.

"Got it." I waited for a second to figure out the little girl's trajectory, and moved quickly, timing the swing of my tomahawk with its rush. The axe head slammed into the girl's forehead, wrenching her off her feet and dumping her on the ground. I kept going, zeroing in on an older zombie that reached out towards me. I batted aside the arms and jammed my knife under its chin, poking the tip out of the top of its greasy head. As it fell, the knife got stuck, so I left it there, going after the next one with just my axe.

This one was dressed well for a zombie. It wore what might have been a tuxedo, complete with wilted brown flower in its lapel. I jumped forward, kicking it in the chest, and knocked it into another zombie dressed in a similar fashion. As I killed the two of them by spiking their heads, I wondered briefly if we hadn't somehow crashed a zombie wedding. If the bride showed up, I would know for sure.

A brief glance showed Jake was doing well by himself, changing things up here and there by jumping in the air before smashing their heads in. I watched him as he jumped up, knocked over a zombie, then stood on its helpless form as he killed another, then swung down quickly to kill the zombie struggling beneath him.

The last two on my side used to be women, and they wore identical dresses. That reinforced the notion that there must have been a wedding nearby. I personally had never seen a wedding that involved more than six people, but I had seen pictures of some pretty lavish affairs.

These two were pretty gross, and I had to be creative killing them, since they came right at me side by side. I ducked under the arms of the one on the left, giving her a shove as she went by, knocking her into her companion. Usually that worked, but somehow the second stayed on her feet and came right after me. I had to jog a little ways away and kill her with a blow to the top of her head. The other one was just getting to her feet, but I didn't give her a chance, I just slammed the 'hawk across her head and killed her for good.

Jake was finished with his side, polishing off another tuxedo zombie. I cleaned my axe and retrieved my knife, pulling it out of the zombie's head with a wet, sucking sound. I used some kerosene to burn off the virus, and did the same with my tomahawk.

"Think I killed a bride and groom over here," Jake said. Sure enough, a zombie in a dirty white dress was slumped over a tipped garbage can.

"I got the rest of the wedding party, then," I said. "And the flower girl. Wonder what happened to cause all this at once?" I asked.

Jake looked over the parking lot. "I'd say a mess of zombies attacked a wedding reception at the hotel, and since the group had nowhere to run, they all died together."

I looked at Jake. That was pretty detailed, and Jake wasn't known for his imagination. "How do you figure? Maybe they were on their way to a reception and someone turned in the limo."

"Oh, I'd say the fifty or so nicely dressed zombies coming out of the hotel is a pretty good clue," Jake said, pointing with his mace.

I looked, and sure enough, they were coming out of the hotel, lurching, stumbling, and dragging themselves in our general direction. They looked pretty bad, being dead for so long, but they were no less deadly for it.

"I think I'll skip the buffet this time," I said, putting my weapons away.

"Right behind you."

We bolted for the truck, hoping there weren't any fast ones to cut us off. We knew when there was a time to fight, and a time to run, and this definitely qualified as a time to run. The entire reception turned as one to follow our flight, and if we had been trapped into a fight, it would have been the end. No matter what the braggarts said, unless the conditions were ridiculously in your favor, you will lose to a horde of zombies. Dad never really talked about his exploits, but others had, and I always figured them to be ninety percent exaggeration.

Jumping in the truck, we sped away, racing back towards Route 50. About halfway there, Jake slammed on the brakes, cursing.

"Dammit!" he yelled.

"What? What's the problem?" I looked for an animal or something that might have run out in front of us.

"I left the cigarettes behind." Jake checked his rear view mirror, and then looked around, possibly checking for a place to turn around.

I held out my hand. "No fucking way are we going back for the damn cigarettes."

Jake ignored me, and I finally put my hand on the wheel. "*No*, Jake."

Jake looked over at me. "That's money we're just leaving behind."

I returned the look. "Better that than our lives. Where's your head?"

Jake looked ruefully at his mirrors.

"Could we check back later? Maybe when the zombies have wandered off?"

"No!"

"Fine." Jake stepped on the gas again and we found Route 50 again. Heading south, we didn't say much until we were a mile or two out of Monee.

"I wasn't really going back," Jake said.

"Uh, huh."

"Really."

"Uh, huh."

Jake was silent for a bit. "Okay, maybe I was. But I didn't."

I looked over at Jake. "You mean, you weren't going to be able to."

Jake looked back. "What?"

"That wheel wasn't turning. Not a chance," I said. I meant it, too. I would have fought Jake to keep from getting myself killed.

It was Jake's turn to say it. "Uh, huh."

CHAPTER 20

I decided to change the subject, since the inside of a truck wasn't the appropriate place for a pissing contest. "What's the address of where we're going?"

Jake took the hint. "It's supposed to be on the outside of town, at a farmhouse."

I looked around. "I hope there's more to it than that." We were in the middle of farm country and there were dozens of farms around. Problem was, if we had to check them all, it would take forever, since they were so damn far apart. This far south, these farms weren't just a hundred or so acres. They were acres measured in thousands.

"Here, look for yourself. This is what I was told." Jake handed me a small slip of paper, which read 'County Highway 20. South Side. First farm past North Peotone Road'.

"All right. Well, you'd better pay attention, because we just passed County Highway 20," I said, pointing at the road sign as it went by.

"Damn."

Jake stopped the truck and reversed course, swinging us onto the right road. We had to be careful going over the tracks, since the winters had twisted the hell out of things lately.

On 20, we passed house after house, and farm after farm. These farms were smaller, but still impressive. Each one had a number of outbuildings, and looked to be quite capable of sustaining themselves. A quick barricade could make these places islands of safety. I didn't understand why people would leave here.

At least, I didn't understand until we crossed over Interstate 57. Then it became clear. Literally hundreds of cars had left the highway, many with their doors still open. I could see tracks in the dirt from cars escaping victims, and wondered where did they have to go? Out into the country, where the farmers had little defense against the oncoming storm? Not a good situation for anybody.

On the other side of 57, we paid attention this time and saw the sign for North Peotone Road. The way ahead was clear, and I could see quite a ways.

"That's it," I said, pointing to a farm positioned relatively close to the main road, unusual for a farm.

"Got it," Jake said, slowing the truck down and angling for the driveway. The grass had grown waist high, and I could see there were several outbuildings to the farm. A huge barn reared up out of the trees to the south, and a big silver silo dominated the yard to the west. An oak tree dominated the southern part of the yard, and a rusty bell stood on a pole near the porch of the house. The house was in remarkably good shape, all things considered, with none of the windows broken, and the doors were still in place. I was very hopeful we would find what we were looking for and be out fairly quickly.

Jake parked the truck and we stepped out. Tall grass always made me nervous, since it was hard to see a zombie in the grass. I didn't want the first warning of a hidden ghoul to be it sitting up and biting me in the nuts. I thought about it, and decided to bring my M1A. Jake cocked an eyebrow at me, but pulled out his rifle as well.

"Just in case our friends from the tracks happen to be in the neighborhood and want to say hi," I explained.

Jake nodded and then said. "You want the house or the buildings?"

"What do you mean?"

"For the desk. For all we know, it's an antique they stored in the loft of the barn."

"Good point. God, I hope not," I said, looking at the size of the barn.

"Your choice," Jake said.

"I'll take the house," I said, figuring it would be easier to be in one place than hunting around several buildings.

"You suck," Jake said sulkily, heading off to the garage.

"Don't give me a choice next time, dope," I laughed, stepping onto the porch. I looked into the windows, trying to see as much as I could before going in. The big room looked like it was full of antiques, so I may hit jackpot right away. There was a big bookcase in the room, so the books we may have wanted would likely be there.

I walked off the porch and around to the front of the house. The entire area was still, no sound, no wind, no anything. It was very peaceful, all things considered.

At the front, I looked into the parlor windows, but didn't see any desk. That was okay, it might be in another room. I would find it when I went inside. I walked around the house some more, looking into windows, but didn't see anything that was going to be a problem.

I was just about to open the kitchen door when I caught something in the corner. It was a shoe, and by the angle it was to the floor, someone's foot was still inside it. I tapped on the door, watching the foot, but it didn't move. I banged a little harder, but the foot stayed put.

Not much in the way of choices. I slung my rifle over my arm and pulled out my tomahawk. While my rifle was useful, firing inside small places really hurts my ears, and I tried to avoid it as much as possible.

I tried the door handle and was pleasantly surprised to find it unlocked. I opened the door and kept my eyes on the foot. It never moved, even when I circled around the table in the small kitchen. I snuck a look outside, and saw Jake working his way through the tall grass towards the barn. I guess the garage was a bust.

On the far side of the table, in front of a pantry, I could finally see the owner of the foot. It was an older gentleman, long dead, slumped back in a chair. A rifle was between his legs, and the man's head was back, revealing his neck, which showed a wound under his chin. His left arm was on the table, and I could see the faint outline of a bite mark on his wrist.

Same old story. We had seen this hundreds of times. Someone gets bit, they find a gun, and they kill themselves before they turn. Can't say as I blame them. I'd probably do the same, if I couldn't find anyone to do it for me.

I pulled the rifle out and looked it over. It was a .22 Anschutz-Savage; at least that's what it said on the barrel. I didn't know if this was the .22 rifle we were looking for, but I put it by the door anyway.

Leaving the body where it was, I looked into the main room. There was a large stairwell leading up, and a couple of rooms to the north and east. I looked into the north room first, and found a bunch of books lining the shelves. Scanning the books quickly, I found the volumes we were supposed to look for and brought them to the table. They were a collection of Mark Twain novels and collected stories, and at first glance, they didn't seem to be anything special besides old.

The other room was a dining room, and there wasn't anything in there. A small bathroom off the main room was the only other area to check, and then I made my way upstairs to check the bedrooms. At the top of the stairs was the main bedroom, and it looked fairly normal, except for the dead woman lying in the bed. She was kind of sprawled back, and I could see she had been shot in the head. There was a little bit of black around her lips and teeth, and I began to understand what might have happened here. This woman was probably the wife of the man downstairs, and when she got sick, she bit him. He killed her, and then killed himself. The question that popped into my mind was who sent us here to collect artifacts, then?

Shrugging, I checked the other rooms quickly. In one, I found another .22 rifle, this one was an old, beat up single shot, with bent sights and a rusty barrel. Following a hunch, I took the beater downstairs and put it next to the nicer one.

The last place I checked was the pantry, and to my surprise, there was a flight of stairs tucked in the back. The stairs were tall and narrow, and I was shocked to find myself in the attic when I reached the top. Those must have been what were once referred to as servant's stairs. I had read about them when we were reading our history books.

The attic was a pretty neat place, with four windows looking out towards each of the cardinal directions. Out of the north, I could see our truck and the countryside we had come through. On the east, I could make out the bridges of the interstate. To the west was another farmhouse, and to the south I could see the silo, the barn, and Jake coming back to the house through the yard.

I could also see two small zombies moving quickly through the grass, heading right for Jake.

CHAPTER 21

Shit! I pulled on the window, but the stupid thing had been nailed shut years ago. Why the hell they would nail a window shut was completely beyond me. I didn't have time to play with it, so I just took the barrel of my rifle and ever so gently busted the glass on one of the panes. I aimed quickly; lining up a shot where I thought the little bugger was going to be and waited for them to fill the sights. It didn't take long for the first one, and just as Jake was saying 'Hey, Aaron!' I let fly with a thirty-caliber bullet.

The sound was loud in the yard, and the little zombie's head burst apart as the bullet killed it. Jake, fully aware now, sprinted for the porch while I tried to get a bead on the second one. That little sucker was proving hard to kill, since it darted around a small stone shed trying cut Jake off. Jake made it to the porch, then turned around and faced the yard, watching for any movement.

I sprinted down the stairs, which was pretty dangerous given how strangely they were constructed. I actually had to jump the last four steps, landing hard in the pantry and slamming into the shelves. I bounced off the shelves and damn near went down another flight of stairs that led to the basement.

I raced for the back door, opening it just in time to see Jake fire once, sending a bullet through the neck of the charging zombie, putting it out of commission.

"Nice shot," I said.

"Thanks," Jake replied. "And thanks for the warning; those little suckers would have nailed me for sure if you hadn't got the first one."

"No problem. Think we might have stirred up any more?" I scanned the tall grass for movement, but couldn't see anything that I couldn't pin on the wind.

"Probably. We're going to have to move fast. Did you find anything in the house?" Jake asked.

"I did find two .22s I didn't know which one we were supposed to get. I also found the books we were looking for. Did you find the roll-top desk?" I secretly hoped he didn't because with the zombie kids and the ghosts of the people who died here looking around at us, I was anxious to leave.

"I did. There's a small apartment in the loft area of the barn, but we should be able to use the hay bale pulleys to get the desk down." Jake said.

"All right, let's get moving. I'd like to be back to some form of civilization before nightfall."

"Let me get the truck," Jake said, moving off the porch and around to the front.

I went inside and pulled together our collection, putting the books in a paper sack and the rifles were rolled up in a newspaper. Jake pulled up and I climbed in, hoping we wouldn't get attacked before we could get the desk out.

We pulled around the silo and Jake moved the truck backwards through the large barn doors. I couldn't see much, but the cursory look I gave to my surroundings told me this was an old barn, one that was old enough to have its own personality, one that would manage this crisis without too much trouble.

Jake parked the truck near a thin flight of stairs and pulled the big door shut. That was a lesson learned the hard way. Too many times people thought they were safe just by being inside, but then the zombies wandered in the open front door.

I went upstairs to look around, and it was kind of weird. The hayloft had been converted to an open-air study. There was bookshelves, a table with three chairs, lamps, and the roll-top desk. There was a typewriter on a small folding table, and a laptop sitting on the recliner. It looked like a nice little getaway for writing or reading, but it was totally out of place for a barn. In the winter, especially the ones we've had over the last few years, this place would be a freezer.

Jake came up the ladder holding the end of the rope attached to the pulley. We pushed the desk over to the edge of the loft and tied off the desk. Jake went down to the other end of the rope, and at his first pull, managed to lift himself off the ground.

I couldn't help but laugh. "Need some more lunch, Jake?"

"You try it, smarty," Jake said, holding the rope out.

I went downstairs, hoping I could actually do it, just to show up Jake a little. However, when I took the rope and gave it a tentative tug, I knew this wasn't going to be easy. I found that a little odd, since we could move the thing on the loft pretty easily. Nevertheless, I had to give it a serious try, so I heaved and managed to move the desk about a foot. But I couldn't do better, so I had to put it down.

"Uh huh," Jake said. "Let's try this one together."

We both took the rope and gave it a hard, steady pull. The desk lifted off the loft and swung precariously over the open space. We let it down quickly, mostly because it was heavy, but also because we weren't sure if the old pulley could hold that much weight. We'd have to risk it for the truck, though.

"All right, let's get it on and out of here." Jake said. We lifted the desk again, and when it got to a certain height, Jake got into the truck and backed it under the desk. We lowered it onto the bed and we were congratulating ourselves as we tied it off.

"Why can't Chicago ever be this easy?" I said, looping a piece of rope around a desk leg.

"Now you've done it. We'll probably blow a tire on our way back to the capital," Jake said, tying off his end.

"Probably," I conceded.

We secured the desk as well as we could, and then cautiously opened the door. The yard was still empty, although there could have been fifty little zombies hiding in the grass and we never would have seen them. Jake moved cautiously through the yard, not just because of any danger to us from zombies, but he also didn't want to drive over some piece of debris that punctured our tires. That would definitely take second place for ruining our day.

We pulled out of the drive and back onto the road. I was for taking the highway back, but Jake said he wanted to go a different way. I pointed out that the sun was going down and we were going to have to find someplace to spend the night. Jake argued that we could spend the night away from the highway, and reduce the risk of any zombie attacks. I had no argument against that, so I agreed, watching as Jake turned towards the west and started driving.

We turned up Route 45, and I knew enough of the area to realize we were taking a straighter route, if slower, than the highway. The area was still largely deserted, even though the number of attacks and outbreaks had dropped of significantly in the last few years. What Jake and I encountered in Peotone was more of the exception rather than the rule. Of course, looking back on it, we just left a big bunch of zombies out in the open, with no place to go but towards populated areas.

I mentioned that to Jake and he was silent for a moment. After a minute, he gave his solution.

"When we drop off the collection, we'll let the heads of the army know, and they can dispatch a platoon to take care of them," Jake said.

That sounded a whole lot better than the two of us going back and trying to take them on ourselves, so I quickly agreed.

We pulled up towards the town of Frankfort, and this particular town was reviving, after years of abandonment. Frankfort had been far enough away from the interstates to avoid the crush of refugees and infections, but the second wave hit it and the people had fled. Our uncles had been the ones who led the push south and cleared the town out without destroying it. Considering what we've heard about our Uncle Duncan, that was rather impressive.

We stopped at a small restaurant, and we shrugged off the curious looks of the patrons. Not many of them had seen specimens like us recently, and a couple whispered the dreaded word 'outbreak' to startled gasps and sharp intakes of breath.

Jake and I sat against the wall, looking over the customers and mentally cataloguing them. Most, I put down as secondary survivors. They were alive simply because they were lucky. Others were more hardcore, wearing their weapons with them, or having firearms on their hips. They must live further out of town, or on the very fringe of the grey lands.

The waitress-slash-owner came over and smiled at us. "Well, what have you been up to?" she asked as we played a little with our drinks.

Jake smiled back. "Collecting. What's the special?" Jake spoke just loud enough to be heard by most of the customers. If we were really lucky, we wouldn't be bothered.

"Collecting, huh?" The waitress, a pretty brunette with a nice smile, made big eyes at Jake, to which that worthy just rolled with it. "Anything of any consequence?"

"Nope. Just the desk and some books, couple of little rifles. Nothing anyone couldn't go out and find in ten minutes anyway. But before we order, Jake said quietly, "Is there a way to speak to the sheriff or deputy, or anyone in charge?"

The woman, whose nametag read Doreen, looked strangely at Jake before answering. "What might you want her for?"

"Need to let her know she might have a problem coming up from the south if she's not paying attention," Jake said.

As soon as the words left his lips, you could feel the air in the room change. One minute, people were spooning in their mouths the next bite; the following moment, people were straining their ears to hear the latest happening.

"Outbreak?" Doreen's voice quivered and I very nearly told everyone to relax, but Jake gave me a small shake of his hand.

"No, not like that," Jake said. "Nothing so serious. But it could get bad if people weren't paying attention, and then we have the big mess all over again. Can we order now?"

After placing our order, I noticed several customers head out quickly, and I was pretty certain the sheriff was going to know about the collectors in her jurisdiction sooner rather than later. That was okay with me, I would rather she come to me than have to chase her down ourselves.

We ordered and ate well when our food arrived. Many of the customers were enjoying their coffee way beyond what someone might consider normal, and I figured they were hoping to see a show.

When our meal was finished, Jake and I stood up to leave. The sheriff hadn't bothered to show up, so I figured she was okay with whatever happened. The rest of the customers watched as we stood up, and as we were leaving, we ran into a beautiful redhead, wearing a uniform and a badge.

"Well, well. The collectors, right?" Her tone was very belligerent, and I knew that was going to cause problems, especially with Jake. Her name badge read 'Brooks', her very blue eyes stared hard at Jake and myself. "Heard there were a couple of you in town. Here's a warning so we know where we stand right away. Your kind isn't welcome here, and if I catch you breaking into any building, be it private or public, I may decide to forego the necessity of due process and just handle you myself." I had no doubt she would, too, but only if Jake and I were unarmed, and we were never fully unarmed.

Jake's tone was low and deliberate, just as it always is when he's about to unload on someone.

"Listen carefully, as I hate to repeat myself, *Brooks,*" Jake said. "We have never broken into any building that wasn't in a grey or black zone, and in those areas, no one lives to protest. This is why we are asked to go into them. No one else will. We have never stolen anything; we have never kept anything we were sent to get. There are unscrupulous collectors out there, but we aren't them. And before you think you can *handle* us, Brooks, keep in mind we've made over thirty runs into the city itself, and we're still here."

There was low murmuring as Jake relayed that information, and I could see Officer Brooks rethinking her position. It was one thing to bluster and threaten young punks and goofy teens. It was another completely when the person you were trying to push was someone who willingly went into the worst of the zombie zones and came back out alive. That person would likely take your threat and shove it down your throat.

Brooks didn't back down, and showed remarkable stupidity. "You've been warned." She stuck out a finger and poked Jake in the chest, emphasizing her point by jabbing him with each word. "I catch you, I deal with you."

Jake, who isn't known for his temperament, grabbed her hand and twisted it inward, causing a gasp of pain to come from Officer Brooks' startled face. She tried to reach across her body for her firearm, but Jake just stepped back, increasing pressure on her wrist, eliciting a cry of pain as Brooks went down to one knee. Jake took a step around the downed officer's leg and brought her hand up behind her head.

Several men stood up to offer help, but I whipped out my pistol and clarified the situation. "She started it, gents. It's a private affair." The look on my face left nothing to the imagination. I would not hesitate to shoot.

Officer Brooks was game. In a burst of energy, she brought her hand over her head, twisting herself so she could strike at Jake's crotch. Jake was ready, and brought the hand he still held straight up. With his other hand, he pushed her elbow, putting the woman's face down onto a chair. I could hear her heavy breathing, and I knew we could probably never come back to this place.

Jake brought his head down to the officer's. "Nice move. But the one who taught you that was my mother. And she taught me more." Jake released Brooks' hand and let her get up. Officer Brooks was sweating, and slowly brought her arm and wrist around to massage them both.

"You're Sarah's son? Then you're..."

Jake cut her off. "I'm Jake. Just Jake. Nothing more." The darkness behind Jake's eyes did not allow for elaboration. "You didn't know."

"You must be Aaron." Brooks had turned to me.

I shook my head. "Not the time. We'll get out of your hair."

Jake nodded and we headed for the door. I kept my gun out but pointed down, just in case.

"Wait!" Officer Brooks held up a hand.

Jake sighed. "What now? An insult you forgot earlier?"

Brooks' face darkened, but I couldn't tell if it was embarrassment or anger.

"Where is this outbreak, or potential outbreak? You can't drop that and walk away."

Jake shook his head. "Watch me."

With that, we were out the door.

CHAPTER 22

We spent the night in an abandoned café off of route 30. Jake and I were both in foul moods, so we didn't bother to talk much at all. I knew Jake had a lot of things on his mind, and the encounter with Officer Brooks didn't help to make things better. During the night, I woke to see Jake standing at the window of the café, just looking out. I almost asked him then what was wrong, but figured he would tell me in his way.

In the morning, we pulled out, and Jake seemed almost back to his normal self. I could tell he was still out of sorts, but there was something in him today, something that was driving him. I knew I would never be able to get it out of him, so I figured I would do what our father did when he wanted us to confess something or to tell him what was on our minds.

I just sat back, stayed quiet, and listened. We turned up a side road, and drove north. The road was just called 80th Avenue, and it would through a couple of subdivisions. Many of the homes had been burned down, and large swaths of land had been cleared for farming. Big hills surrounded the farms, and from experience I knew those hills were actually debris piles that had been reclaimed by nature. If you dug into them, you'd find all kinds of stuff.

We turned down a long driveway and headed towards what looked like a school. It had been long abandoned, but it seemed like a decent place, still. The windows were intact, although the caulking around them was cracking. In a few years and another hard winter, and this place would begin the long slide into oblivion.

Jake pulled into the parking lot, being careful not to bump into the dividers that lay hidden under foliage. I had no idea why we were here, but since I wasn't driving, I was pretty much just an observer.

"How come we're here?" I asked as Jake stopped the truck. He got out without answering and started walking towards the building. Not having anything else to do and unable to get answers from the dashboard, I got out and followed Jake.

At the front of the building, Jake just stopped and looked around. I caught up to him and looked around myself. The building was in good shape, someone could actually move in here and save it with little trouble, but if no one did, in a few years it would start to decay and crumble. The windows were tinted, but if I looked close, I could see boards and curtains covering the lower floors. The upper floors had no need of such protection. We walked around the building, I noted the plywood on the south doors, and the wood in the windows of an oddly shaped room attached to the back of the building. Across the field, up near what used to be a baseball field, was a large patch of dirt where nothing grew. It was very strange, but not as strange as the collection of crosses which made up a small graveyard on another side yard.

We completed our tour and wound up back in the front. Jake and I hadn't spoken the whole time, and I got the impression he wanted me to see everything before he gave his reasons for stopping here.

"Do you know what this place is?" Jake said, with a small smile on his face.

"Without any other clues, I'm going to say this is a school, and one that was used in the past as a safe place when the zombies first appeared." I said, figuring to be about eighty percent right.

"On the surface, you're right," Jake said. "But it's more than that. Uncle Tommy told me about this place."

Our Uncle Tommy was a great one for stories and for training. He was your average, quiet guy, but unbelievably steady in the face of just about anything. He rarely got riled up, and was a source of good humor when his best friend Duncan was around. I was curious now as to the connection of this place to our uncle.

"What is this place, then?" I asked.

Jake looked almost wistful. "This is where Dad and our uncles made their stand. This is where they fought back for the first time. According to Uncle Tommy, they fought off nearly a thousand zombies here. And that was on the first day."

I had to admit I was stunned. Not because I didn't believe it could be done, but because I suddenly had the sneaking suspicion the stories about our father might actually be true. Dad never talked about what he had done during the War on the Zombies. He always said it didn't matter, just worry about today and tomorrow, not yesterday. Everything we had ever heard about what he and his crew had done, we always got from secondhand sources. However, we always suspected those stories were elaborated to make good telling. I never thought they might have happened for real.

"Damn." I wasn't going to win marks for eloquence anytime soon, but it summed up everything I was feeling pretty well.

"Yeah." Jake must have been in the same contest. "Let's get moving. There's another place I want to see."

"Where?"

"On our way to the capital, don't worry." Jake had decided to be mysterious, which I would allow for this little adventure. If it made him less of a grouch, I was all for trips down memory lane. On the other hand, I was a little perturbed that Jake knew about this and had kept it to himself. In addition, I think I was mad at my uncles for talking to Jake and not to me.

We drove up 80th Avenue and as we passed by a condo complex, Jake pointed out that Dad had moved everyone there to get them out of the school.

"Why? The school seems like a perfectly good place to stay safe," I argued, not seeing the point of trying to re-establish a safe haven when one already existed.

"I asked that same question, and Uncle Tommy said Dad wanted people to be somewhere familiar, somewhere they could live, not just be alive. It was the thing that kept him going, all those years back," Jake said.

"Rumor has it you were the thing that kept him going," I said, wondering what kind of reaction I would get. While Jake apparently had spoken to our uncles, I had some questions I had answered by our mother.

Jake stiffened slightly. "Yeah, well not anymore, it seems." He stopped talking after that and I regretted my words. I think

Jake was taking our father's absence much harder than I had previously thought.

CHAPTER 23

We travelled up the main route towards the capital, stopping briefly to fill up our tank with gas. We saw many signs of life around here, people who went back to their homes after several years, and others who took up residences that were no longer claimed. Many homes had been burned down, and the result was a lot of open space for small farms and orchards. The one benefit of the apocalypse was the shift in thinking from 'all about me' to 'we're in this together.' The sad part was it took nearly the extinction of the human race to realize it.

We passed by the big mall in the middle of Orlan, and it was a sad sight to see. A few years ago, teenagers had taken over the big mall, mostly teens who had been orphaned by the Zombie War. At last unofficial count there had been nearly three hundred living there, enjoying themselves and pretty much doing as they pleased. One winter, though, the roof collapsed, killing two hundred of them, and scattering the rest. Jake and I had been part of the search for survivors, and I will never forget pulling those bodies out of the rubble, especially the little ones, for several of the teens had had children. I remember Jake had openly wept for the babies. That was the last time I had actually seen him cry.

Past the mall, things spread out a bit, but Jake took a turn in the opposite direction of the capitol.

"Another trip down memory lane?" I asked dryly.

"This one is for both of us," Jake said.

"How so?" This was different and I let my tone show it.

"I went into Dad's room last month," Jake said.

In a way, I was mad, but my curiosity overcame my anger. "All right, if you force me, I'll ask. What did you find?" We had stayed out of dad's room ever since we found the note that told us he was gone. At first, it was out of anger, but then it became a sign of respect. Lately, though, it was becoming an obsession, as our father was gone longer and longer.

Jake smiled at me. "Not much. He left a box for me and some instructions. There was a box for you, as well. And before you ask, no I didn't look. You can when we get back."

"What did yours say?" I asked, very anxious now to get home.

"That's for me to know, as yours is for you. But there was something for both of us, and this little side trip is part of it," Jake said. "Ah, here it is."

We turned down a road and went into a little valley, crossing some railroad tracks and heading up a hill. Jake turned the truck into another subdivision, and by this time, I was thoroughly confused as to the reason for this trip.

The truck wound through a living community, with several homes occupied and many people out and about. That was the front of the subdivision. When we crossed another street, it was as if someone had turned off a switch. There wasn't any children playing about, there weren't any people going about their daily chores, not a single house looked occupied. Some of the homes looked to have been looted, and many others were just dilapidated husks, waiting for that one severe storm to finally bring them down.

At the end of the street, we pulled into the driveway of a modest, two story home. It had a brick first floor and a second floor covered in grey siding. It looked to be perfectly normal, except for the unkempt grass and bushes around the house. The first floor windows were nearly obscured by evergreen bushes that had gone unchecked, and the lilies around the drain spout were out of control to the point they covered half the side yard. The neighbors' yards weren't in any better shape, and the tall trees by the sides and front of the house could use some serious pruning.

"This it?" I asked. "Where are we?"

Jake smiled that little annoying smile of his. "Hang on, I'll let you know. It took me a week to find a map that would lead me to this place."

I could believe that. Maps were somewhat scarce, and a good set of roadmaps were hard to come by. Maps that showed details of streets were even rarer. Once upon a time, people just turned on their computers or phones and were able to get directions with little effort. We had landline phones these days, and I had heard there was some progress with cell towers, whatever those were. But no maps to be had.

Jake and I walked around the house, passing through the tall gate for the fenced back yard. In the back, we were a little surprised at what looked to be an incomplete porch. Some projects never got finished.

Looking in the windows, we couldn't see much. The windows were slightly higher than normal, and there seemed to be boards covering the windows. That was interesting. I wondered what we would find when we went inside.

Circling back to the front, Jake and I stood on the front porch. I tried the door, and was unsurprised to find it locked. I was about to pull a small crowbar out of my pack when Jake surprised the hell out of me by producing a key.

Jake looked at me and shrugged. "It was with the note." He tried the key, and with a little wiggling, the old lock gave up the fight and relented. Jake pushed the door open and waited a second. When we didn't hear anything, we went inside.

The house was very neat and tidy, sparsely furnished but tasteful. The wood floors and furniture had a layer of dust, but looked undisturbed after all these years. We walked carefully, making sure we didn't kick up too much dust. The air was stale and musty, and not easy to breathe.

In the kitchen, we found a lot of interesting stuff. Several maps were laid out on the table, and the counter had a lot of supplies that looked as if they had been fussed over, and then left, for whatever reason. Jake went over to the casement windows above the sink and opened them. Since the front door was open, the wind rushed through the house, taking all the stale air out and replacing it with sweet-smelling air.

Problem was that wind stirred up the dust, and we were coughing and choking for a few minutes while the dust cleared out.

"Glad you did that?" I coughed at Jake.

"Not really," He coughed back.

"Mind if I hazard a guess?" I asked.

"About what?"

"This used to be Dad's house, before things went south all over," I said.

Jake nodded. "In the note he left me, he gave me the address and the key, saying when I felt I was ready I could go take a look." Jake looked around. "Not sure what I was supposed to be ready for, though."

"Well, let's look around. Maybe we'll find what he's talking about," I said. We agreed to split up, and I went upstairs while Jake went downstairs. I had noticed the windows of the first floor had been boarded up, and I realized that the wood was from the deck. Pretty smart thinking, there. Upstairs, the windows were left alone, except for the blinds, which were down and angled to let in light, but nothing could see in from the street. I was gaining respect for my father as he dealt with the undead when they first arrived.

In a room that could only be a baby's, I checked the closets and found nothing of interest. A couple of side rooms had nothing either, save for a desk and a guest bed. The master bedroom was cozy, but dusty. I wasn't going to open the window and cause a dust storm, thank you.

Finding nothing except some clothing, I headed back downstairs. I could hear Jake coming up from the basement, and I would guess he had found nothing either. The house was very utilitarian, and everything of use in an evacuation had been taken.

It wasn't until I reached the landing at the bottom of the stairs that I saw it. Had I not gone upstairs, we would have passed it right on by. I didn't see it as I went up, and we didn't see it when we came in, but it was there, nonetheless.

It was a picture of a family, taken by someone who liked close ups. I recognized my dad, and the baby in the picture had to be Jake, since it had his eyes and features. But the woman threw me for a loop. I looked long and hard at the picture, taking it off the wall and examining it in better light. I wiped off the dust, but it didn't change the truth of what I was seeing.

The woman wasn't our mother. It wasn't Sarah.

CHAPTER 24

I took the picture to the family room, where Jake was running his hand over the wood that covered the windows. I wondered if the note from our father had mentioned what I was seeing.

"Jake?"

He turned to face me. "What's up? Find something?"

I handed him the picture, and he first looked at it and smiled. But the smile turned to a frown and then Jake pulled a chair out and sat down.

"Jesus," He said. He looked down at the picture. He studied it for a long time.

I didn't say anything, understanding that this was Jake's moment alone. I stepped back and went into the study next to the kitchen. There was a computer, and piles of notes and maps. I looked over the notes, and smiled as I read how our father had learned about the dead, and how to beat them. That was Dad . As much as he denied it, he was a planner.

I went back to the kitchen, and Jake was standing. He was looking out the window, holding the picture at his side.

"You okay?" I asked. I knew it was a hell of thing to discover, and I wasn't sure how Jake was going to take it.

Jake looked at me. "Not really. I came here expecting to find some sort of answers, but instead, I leave with more questions. And the one guy who can explain it all to me is probably a thousand fucking miles away!"

I had to admit he had a point. "What do you want to do?"

"Let's get the crap back to the capital, get paid, and get home. We'll figure out what we want to do from there." Jake said, heading for the door.

"Good enough." I said. I was anxious to get home. I wanted to know what surprises my father had for me in the box he had left. Hopefully I wouldn't find out I had another father.

Jake was quiet on the way home and I couldn't blame him. I had no idea what I would do if I found out the person I thought was my mother really wasn't, and what had happened to my real mother? A worse question, and one that was probably going through Jake's head, was whether our father had killed his mother. With the end of the world and all, it was a real possibility.

We drove towards the capital, reaching the outskirts pretty quickly. Jake drove towards the big food market, and parked the truck in a spot easily accessible. There weren't too many vehicles out and about, but the ones that were available were well taken care of. It wasn't like anyone was making any more of them.

Jake got out, and I met him around the back.

"Where are we supposed to drop this thing off?" I asked, not relishing the thought of trying to lift the heavy thing off the bed of the truck.

Jake checked his notes. "Says here that we are to park it anywhere, go to this address, and let them know it's here. They will take care of the rest."

I thought about it for a minute. "All right then. You want to be the one to go get them, or stay here?"

Jake shook his head. "I'll go get them. Quiet reflection isn't going to help me much right now."

I understood. "I'll be here then."

Jake walked off and I had little else to do but hang out. There were a lot of kids in the marketplace today, and since I was a stranger, I was the object of shy attention. Several kids hovered around, staring and whispering to each other, trying to look occupied when I looked directly at them. At one point, I stood up suddenly, scattering several to their respective parents. I chuckled as nervous eyes peeped from around the safe havens of parent legs.

Others were interested in me as well. I could see several teenagers hanging about, trying to look tough and shrugging me off as if I wasn't all that tough. I had seen it before, and it was interesting to see the teens that had lived here all their lives, and the ones that came in from the frontier, where there was a lot bigger threat of zombies. I didn't pay either any attention.

I wandered over to a couple of the tables, spending a few coppers on some fresh fruit for the trip home. I didn't notice the trio of large men headed my way until I was right on top of them.

"Sorry, gents. Didn't see you." I tried to step around, but one of them blocked my way.

"Collector, huh?" The tall blond one said sarcastically, flipping up one of the straps on my pack. I immediately marked him as one to cause serious pain to. The other two spread out a little behind their leader. That was unfortunate for them, since it gave them only one direction to attack from. I noticed that more than a few people were watching to see what I would do.

"Yeah," I said. "It's a living." I started to walk around the guy to get back to the truck, but he stepped into the way.

"Word is, collectors are supposed to be tough." Blondie looked me up and down. "You don't look so tough."

I smiled. "I'm not. I prefer to be lucky." I tried once more to go around the guy, but he stepped into the way again. This time, he actually put his hand on my chest and tried to push me back. He got a concerned look on his face when I didn't move.

"Lucky? Yeah, you'd have to be. You'd couldn't possibly be capable of..."

Whatever he was going to say was lost as I grabbed the collar of his shirt and pulled him towards me. I threw the bag of fruit at the closest guy behind Blondie, and then knelt slightly, taking the big guy across my knee and tossing him to the ground. I whipped out my knife and held it to the throat of the man on the ground, holding a second knife out to deal with anyone foolish enough to charge me.

"Wait! Stop!" Jake's voice cut across the marketplace, as the area had suddenly grown very quiet. Dozens of faces stared at me and the man on the ground, who was desperately trying not to move,as I kneeled on his chest and held a knife on him. Him friends had their hands up and were trying to tell me something.

"I got this, Jake," I said, shifting my eyes down to the man I was on.

"Aaron, stop! It was a supposed to be a joke!" Jake was laughing and I wasn't really sure what was going on, so I decided to let the man up. He climbed slowly to his feet with the help of his friends, and held a hand to his neck. I hadn't hurt him, although I probably had scared the hell out of him.

I turned my attention to Jake. "Explain." One of the men held the fruit out to me and I took it with a scowl.

"These are the guys who have come to get the desk and stuff. I thought it would be funny to get a rise out of you. I didn't think you'd try to kill them," Jake laughed and I had to admit it had worked.

I took a deep breath and looked over at the three men. "No hard feelings?"

Blondie shook his head. "When I saw you, I thought about dumping the whole scheme." He touched his throat again. "Kinda wished I had. No hard feelings. I should have known better than to mess with a collector."

We shook hands and went over to the truck. When the assembled audience realized the show was over, they went back to their shopping. At the truck, the men heaved the desk out of the bed, and I handed over the rifles and books. Blondie checked a list in his pocket, and then spoke.

"Says here only the one rifle. Where did the other one come from?"

I answered. "Found two in the house, didn't know which one was the right one."

"Got no claim to it. You want it?" He asked.

I knew a rifle was decent money and we could have sold it, but I figured I owed it to them for the scare. "No, thanks. I don't care much for suicide guns." I wasn't going to let it go for free, though.

Blondie looked at the rifle, and then shrugged. "I don't believe in curses."

Jake shook his hand. "Me either. You have the balance?"

Blondie nodded and handed over a small pouch of coins. Jake checked the amount, transferred the money to his own pouch, and handed the empty one back.

"Nice doing business with you," Jake said.

The men departed and Jake looked slyly at me. I held up a hand and Jake dutifully stood still as I thumped him on the forehead. He knew his joke had nearly gone seriously wrong and was sorry for it.

"Anything we need?" I asked, looking out at the marketplace.

"Not today," Jake said, climbing into the truck.

I was right behind him. "Let's get home." I wanted to see what my father had left for me, and playing games around here wasn't going to get the job done.

CHAPTER 25

We headed south and picked up the main highway to the West. I-80 was mostly cleared, and we were able to make good time. Instead of heading back through Ottawa, Jake kept going and turned off the road to Utica. This was not a main road, so there had been some cars to avoid, but over the years, we had managed to clear the way. Unlike the other highways, though, there weren't any leftover zombies in these. Our dad and Julia's had made sure of that.

We passed a couple of homes along the way, and were surprised to see one of them occupied. We had no problem with that; people did it all the time. If you could keep a house, you were welcome to it, as long as no one had a prior claim. There had been some incidents in the past where someone went home to find another person living there. It led to some awkward moments, but overall I like to think people were pretty good about it. I mean there were so many empty houses and land out there that we all could have massive estates if we wanted them.

Most people lived in communities and towns, and there were few who chose to live in the frontier as we did. My father had his reasons for choosing Starved Rock and I can't fault him for them. He made his home out in the middle of zombie territory, and fought to keep it. If anyone earned the right to be here, he did.

We pulled into the long drive and up towards the lodge. We passed a ditch and a fence, and finally pulled into the circular drive at the front of the lodge. Julia came out to see us, and gave both of us hug, which surprised Jake as much as it did me.

"Hey, good to see you, too," I said, pulling my gear and guns out of the truck. "How come you're so friendly?"

Julia rocked up on her toes, and then back onto her heels. "Just because. I'm glad you guys are back. It's not the same place when someone's away."

I could accept that. There have been times that I have been alone, and the big place tends to have a lot of noise when you least expect it.

"Well, we were successful, although we had to kill a wedding party to get the job done," Jake said.

Julia's eyes got big and I just laughed. "We'll tell you about it in a minute. I want to take a shower and get my stuff taken care of."

Julia turned to Jake. "You look thoughtful. Anything new?"

Jake gave her a sideways smile. "Yeah, we learned something new. I'll tell you about it later."

Jake walked off and Julia turned to me with questions in her eyes. I shook my head and said, "It's his story to tell, not mine."

Later that evening, after I had showered and changed, I wandered up to the second floor and down the hall, past my bedroom and towards the room my parents had shared. It had been two years since my father had gone, and I hadn't been in here since then. I had often wondered what it would take for a man to leave his children, and I had spent a long time being angry about it. But I have never loved a woman like my dad had loved my mom, and losing someone like that must have been hard to take.

I took a deep breath and opened the door. Since Jake had already been in here, it wasn't as bad as it might have been. The bed was made, and the place was neat. It wasn't even dusty, so Jake must have cleaned a bit. He was weird like that. On the small coffee table in the lounge section of the suite was a small box, about the size of a big shoebox. It was made of wood, and closer inspection revealed it was handmade. The sides were meticulously put together, and on the lid were painted in gold letters 'Aaron'.

I wondered briefly if Jake had a box like this, but I was pretty sure he did. I sat down on the couch and put the box in my lap. It had been made with care and I wanted to appreciate that care. The lid opened without a fuss, and I took a tentative look inside.

To tell the truth, there was a lot less than I had expected. There was a picture of a couple I had never seen before, an old knife in a worn leather sheath, an envelope, a pouch with fifty gold coins in it, and a thick, leather covered journal.

I looked first at the knife with a practiced eye, noting it was razor sharp, with a single edge and a smooth, stacked leather grip. It was as much a fighting knife as I had ever seen. I looked at the picture, and I could recognize some of my father's features on the man. I realized I was looking at a picture of my father's parents, my grandparents. I put the picture down carefully and picked up the journal. It was a thick book, and inside was inscribed, 'My War on the Dead' written by my father.

I looked at the book, and opened a few pages. It had been neatly typed, and there were over eight hundred pages. Dad must have found a computer that worked, and spent a lot of time chronicling what he had gone through. A careful inspection revealed that Dad had also torn out the pages of another book, and glued his inside. Clever that. I had a lot of reading to do.

I opened the envelope last and pulled out the single sheet of a handwritten letter. I couldn't believe I was shaking so bad, and had to settle myself before I picked it up again. I leaned back and began to read.

My son Aaron,

I never thought I might be writing a letter like this, since I always figured I would be the one to go before your mother. But fate had other ideas, and I found myself without an anchor. I had you and your brother, but you two are of an age that you don't need me anymore. That doesn't make me sad, it's the way of things and I think I prepared the two of you as best I could to deal with the world you've inherited.

You have many gifts, Aaron, and as you read this, you need to start finding them are using them. This world has a ton of possibilities for you, and you have the good fortune of learning from the mistakes of the past and making it a good world for generations. That's what you need to do, son. Make the world a better place than it is. Find your way, don't stray from it, and make everything you do focused on your way.

The picture is your grandparents, my mother and father. Your grandmother died in the early stages of the zombie uprising and your grandfather found his way south. You might remember him from when he visited a long time ago. If he's alive still, he might show up on your door someday. His old Marine Ka-Bar knife is there, so use it well. It served him well for twenty years in the Marines. I'm giving you these things so you have a history, a place in the world. So many people just ended, and the rest had to start their histories over. You at least have part of yours.

The book is a record of what I and your uncles went through during the start of the zombies and the wars that followed. It is your history as well. There is also the story of your family, going back to when your great, great, great, great grandparents came over from Europe.

I will return someday, I give you my word. Until then, I want you to do two things. Believe in yourself and become what you are meant to be.

Love to you, my darling boy.

Dad.

I don't know how long I sat there, just reading and re-reading the letter. I didn't want to put it away, because it was all I had of my father. I looked over the journal, and immediately it was precious to me as well. I spent some time looking at the picture of my grandparents, wishing I could have met my grandma. The knife I looked over, and knowing its history, I was sure I would respect what it could do. Doubtless, it had seen as much combat as my own knives had. I stood up and strapped the knife onto my belt, and I was surprised at how easily it slipped into my hand. I looked it over again and it positively glowed with a happy kind of wickedness, as if it was anxious for action.

I put the letter, journal, picture and money back into the box, and left the suite. I felt oddly calm, like a hole in my life had been filled, and yet I had a lot of questions for myself. What was I meant to do? What was I supposed to accomplish?

Was I supposed to apprentice myself? Unfortunately, I had no answers for these questions.

The next morning, Julia came into my room and sat on one of the chairs as I related what I found. She was interested in the journal, and I promised her she could read it as soon as I was done with it.

"We have another job, by the way," Julia said. "Came in this morning."

"Is it a rush? I feel like we've done nothing but jobs for the last three weeks." I laid back and put a hand over my eyes, as if to pretend it didn't exist if I couldn't see it.

"Jake wants to wait a little while, too, so we'll probably go in a week. He says by the look of it, it should be fairly easy. " Julia stood and walked over to the bed, sitting on the far edge. "Anything else in the box?"

"Nothing that has a big impact on our day today." I looked up. "Whose turn is it for making breakfast?"

"Yours. I'm hungry. Get up. Get up. Get up!" Julia slapped my feet and I whipped a pillow at her, knocking her off the bed.

It was probably going to be a good day after all.

CHAPTER 26

"Move your ass, they're right behind me!"

"Where's Julia?"

"She's not here?"

"Oh, God."

"*Run!*"

We bolted down the dark corridor, having discovered that about thirty zombies blocked our exit. Jake had gone ahead to scout, and that hadn't turned out so well.

"Do you think she went into one of the stores?" Jake guessed, as we passed a doorway with a store name painted on it.

"Well, let's see. She's not with me, and she's not with you. I'd rather not think she's languishing in the stomachs of about a dozen zombies, so that would be my hopeful guess." I said. This whole collection was one big nightmare after another. Absolutely nothing had gone right, even from the beginning.

"Don't get morose. Just run, you damn fool," Jake snarled.

I gave it right back. "Watch that 'fool' shit, asshole. You're the jackass that ran in here in the first place."

"You know what? Just shut up." Jake ran headlong into the crash bar on the door to the shopping area of the mall, knocking it open and tripping over a pile of boxes that had been left by the door.

I followed, and as I watched the door close, I could see dozens of glowing eyes coming towards us. I pulled off my pack and quickly rummaged through it. The door conveniently had no handle, so it was going to open easily when the zombies hit it in force. I pulled out a small wooden wedge, and jammed it in the small space between the door and the door jam.

"What's that for?" Jake asked.

"Something Uncle Duncan taught me. Can buy you ten seconds or more when you really need it," I said, tapping the wood with the butt of my pistol.

Jake looked put out. "How come he never taught me that?"

"Probably because you preferred to listen to yourself," I said, not to put too fine a point on it.

Whatever he was going to say was lost as the first zombie plowed into the door. The whole thing shook, and the wedge was nearly knocked out.

"Damn!" I said, pounding it back into the crack. "We gotta get the hell out of here!" I said, backing away from the door.

"Where the fuck is Julia?" Jake said, turning and running down the hall. Storefront after storefront was smashed and looted, although the dust indicated that there had been some time in between visitors.

As if in answer, a single wail drifted to us from the darker recesses of the mall. Jake and I traded looks as we bolted in that direction. The mall was laid out in a cross pattern, with longer halls on the north and south ends. There was a food court in the middle, but that place had long gone to the dust and decay. I had dared Jake to open one of the fridges, but he had impolitely declined.

We had not originally wanted to come to this mall. Malls were generally bad news. Either they were full of zombies, from people trying to take refuge when the original outbreak had occurred, or they had kept the virus out, and had become little communities of their own, with interesting ways of doing things. One mall had a community where the rule was clothing was not allowed. We didn't stay long, although we looked for a while.

This mall was definitely not one of the latter. As we ran down the dark wing, a black groaning shape reared up out of the darkness and confronted me. I barely slowed down as I swung my axe, slamming the blade into the skull of the zombie in front of me. It went down without a twitch and I yanked my 'hawk out as I passed.

Another shape rose up, but it was too slow to intercept me. Jake nailed it with his mace, and we were still moving. As we went deeper into the darkness, we could see a small bit of light coming from a side corridor to the left. We could also see about a half dozen glowing eyes turn our way as we thumped through debris and decay. This mall had definitely seen better days. I think it might have been used as a refuge for about a day, but then people got greedy, looted it, and took off. Then the zombies moved in and there went the neighborhood.

"Baby Gap! Baby Gap!" Jake yelled, and at first I thought he was nuts, but then I saw the sign, and realized he was trying to avoid the horde that was headed our way. I dove sideways and went through a hole in the window, miraculously avoiding cutting the hell out of myself. I rolled out of the way, as Jake dove after me and we both stood up, ready to fight.

Not surprisingly, we heard a noise in the back. Jake nodded to the left and I took the right. We crept past bare shelves and creepy mannequins, trying to stay silent so the horde outside would pass us by. The noise repeated itself, and then there was a curse.

I looked over at Jake and we both nodded. Julia. Stepping quickly to the back counter, we could see a red light flashing back and forth, obviously looking for something. Jake stepped closer and suddenly the light shifted and two feet of sharpened steel flashed past his face.

"Hey!" Jake slipped back and I stepped forward in his place. The blade came towards me, but I knocked it out of the way with my axe.

"Knock it off," I said quietly. "What the hell are you doing in here? You were supposed to have come to the utility door."

I think Julia actually blushed. "I wanted some jeans."

"Are you fucking serious?" Jake asked. "There's about thirty zombies headed this way!"

"Hey, we were always taught to take advantage of opportunities as they presented themselves. Here is a jeans store, why the hell not?' Julia said defiantly.

"Was that you we heard wailing?" I asked, changing the subject.

"Yes, that was me." Julia looked embarrassed again.

"Why, dare I ask?" Jake said.

"I can't find my size." Julia pouted. "There's all kinds of fat people sizes and super-skinny sizes, but nothing in *my* size."

Jake had never been known for his tact. As a matter of fact, his honest nature has caused more fights than a body has a right to. "Well, you could lose weight."

Julia stared daggers at Jake. I was actually surprised he didn't fall dead right there.

"Or gain it to fit in the fat jeans," I tried helpfully with a smile.

Julia turned her gaze on me and I was shocked I didn't disintegrate in a pile of ash. I swear lasers came out of her eyes for a second and singed my eyebrows.

"All right, enough of this," Jake said. "We have about a minute before the ones outside figure out where we wandered off to. We weren't exactly subtle in our choice of entrances to this place."

"Any back exits?" I asked, although I was leery of them since the utility tunnel was such a fun place.

Julia shook her head. "None that I want to use. I definitely heard something when I checked the door."

"Well, what then? We can't get out the back and the front is out of the question. Wait. How did you get here? You didn't go through the window, did you?" I asked Julia.

"I came in through the regular GAP store," Julia said.

"They're connected?" Jake asked.

"Yeah, you passed the connecting corridor to come back here."

"So there could be a whole mess of zombies right around the corner?"

"Suppose so." Julia shrugged. "As long as they don't have a reason to come back here, we should be okay. We can sneak out later."

"Jake?" I asked suddenly.

"What is it, Aaron, I'm trying to get us out of here." Jake sounded exasperated.

"Do mannequins move?"

CHAPTER 27

"Shit!" Jake figured out in a hurry what I was referencing to, and immediately drew his knife for confrontation.

"Got it," I said, moving forward. The zombie, an advance scout for the horde that was milling about in the main hall walked out of the darkness towards me. I couldn't see it all that well, but it's glowing eyes were as clear to me as if it was outside in the sun. I used those eyes as an aiming point and drove the spike end of my tomahawk right between them. The zombie fell backwards, and its outstretched arm caught a display rack, pulling it down against a glass table. The rack shattered the table with a huge crash, sending a shower of broken glass cascading to the tile floor. The sound was a waterfall of tinkling notes, and in the immediate silence following the crash, Jake only had to say one thing.

"*Damn.*"

An ear-splitting chorus of groans flew in from the outside of the store, matched by another chorus coming from ghouls inside the store as well. They were actually a lot closer than I had wanted to admit, so the quiet talking was pretty much over.

I took the lead. "Follow me!" I ran towards the front with Jake and Julia close behind. I could see several dark shapes working their way towards the other door where zombies were already streaming in, and so their attention wasn't on us, thank God.

I grabbed a low display table and heaved it over my head. The thing was a lot heavier than I thought it was, but that would help with what I had in mind. I waited a second for about three or four zombies to be in the line of fire, and then I heaved the table through the window. Since the window had already been broken, the rest went easily with little resistance.

The table crashed into the trio of zombies on the other side, and we were right behind it. We had no room for error in this place. The table did not hit two of the dead, and they came right at us. Jake took a wide swing and literally knocked the one on the right completely off its feet.

Julia was right behind on the one on the left, and the weighted end of her staff swept the legs out from under the zombie who fell as the spear head streaked for its eyes. A quick crunch and the job was done. I was already past the two and heading back the way we had come. The side door was out, a glance back showed dozens of zombies that way, so we had to return through the mess we had run from.

I darted from one side to the other, dodging debris and overturned kiosks. Julia and Jake were right behind me. It was dangerous, since it was fairly dark, and there was a lot of crap on the floor.

In the middle of the center of the mall was a glass elevator. Surrounding that elevator was a defunct waterfall. Long-dried pools had revealed their treasure, coins were all over the bottom of the waterfalls. We didn't stop to pick any up, since there was about five zombies waiting for us under the dull glow of the skylights which illuminated the mall's center court.

I dodged into a jewelry store, hoping to take a side route around the five, and that was when Jake said, "Where..."

I didn't catch the rest since the distraction caused me to slam into a display case. I hit the thing dead center, and it was solid enough to knock me back on my ass. Julia was right behind me, and my sudden stop and fall, caused her to slam into my back and be on the bottom when I sat down.

"OOOOF!" She said as the air left her lungs.

"Sorry!" I rolled off of her and Jake helped us both to our feet. The five in the court headed our way and I ran out of the jewelry store, moving through the scattered tables of a coffee shop. Jake grabbed up one of the chairs as he went by and hurled it at the group. Knocking two of them down, the chair wrapped up the legs of a third.

"Nice!" I called as we raced towards the longer end of the mall. We passed by a couple of stores that looked like they hadn't been looted, but since one was a lingerie store and the other a greeting card store, it wasn't that big of a surprise. No one needed that stuff in a zombie apocalypse.

Passing a Pottery Barn, I moved under a stairwell and skidded to a stop. Several zombies, which must have been inside the stores when we first went by, and were prompted to explore in search of food, blocked our path.

Julia was paying attention this time and avoided running into me. She moved to the left side and Jake moved to the right. The zombies groaned and moved towards us in a group, making things difficult for a fight.

"Call it," Jake said, hefting his weapon.

I very nearly said we should take them when I happened to see movement in the darkness behind the zombies. I couldn't tell how many there were, but the amount of shifting told me there were quite a few.

"Upstairs. Now!" I turned and bolted for the stairs, taking two at a time. I reached the top and ducked under the arms of a zombie that came limping out of a candle store. I stood up and with a swift backswing of my 'hawk, smacked the zombie in the head. It hit the railing and was sufficiently overbalanced that it fell over the side, falling hard to splatter on the floor below.

We were alone for the time being, although the ones we ran from were slowly making their way up the stairs.

"What now?" Julia whispered. Jake was at the top of the stairs, eyeballing the oncoming horde and hefting his weapon. I knew if I didn't get things moving, he'd probably wade into them and start killing.

"There's got to be an exit from the second floor up here." I said, looking for the telltale signs of light from doors and windows. I thought there looked to be some sunlight down the way towards Macy's, but it was hard to tell.

"Well, there isn't one from that side." Julia pointed across the mall chasm to the other side.

"Maybe there's one around this area here." I started in that direction and Jake came up the stairs. I knew if we left this area, we had to be sure, otherwise we were in for a fight to come back this way.

I stepped forward and checked the corner. There wasn't a zombie nearby, but I was hearing some strange things. It sounded like something was bumping into something and couldn't get away. I didn't have the time to check it out, so I moved past it.

At the corner of Abercrombie and the Bedding Experts, two well-dressed zombies stumbled into view. Julia didn't waste time and speared one of them, and Jake hammered the other. I wasn't too worried about what we might encounter as long as they came out in small doses.

We moved forward into the darkness, and I was happy to report to the other two that it looked like we were going to find an exit after all. I could definitely see some light at the end of this tunnel, and for once, that wasn't metaphorical.

I stepped up the pace and approached the corner, stealing a look around, hoping we would be all clear, but I would be okay with a few zombies.

What I wasn't expecting was to come face to face with a ghoul that was slowly working his way along the wall in the opposite direction as myself.

"Whoa!" I said, jerking my head back as the little nasty lunged forward in an attempt to bite my nose off. He reached out and caught hold of my backpack strap, pulling me in for a bite. I slammed a hand up into its throat and forced myself back, keeping the teeth away from my face and wrist. I twisted to the right, slamming the ghoul up against the wall and getting a real good look at it. It was male, like I thought, and it was sparsely dressed in a pair of long shorts and a t-shirt. The t-shirt was streaked with black, and the zombie grabbed and pulled at me with its other arm, latching onto my other strap. I increased my push and felt my hand start to slip on the dead skin that was shifting under my grip.

I squeezed hard, feeling the dead thing's throat and bones, and I wished I had the strength to crack its neck. The dead face snapped and groaned at me, opening its maw and it tried to take a huge bite out of my face.

I couldn't get it to release its grip, and I dared not release mine, so I had to do the next best thing, and that was to draw my grandfather's knife and try for a kill. Trouble was, my angle was wrong, thanks to the zombie's arm that was holding my strap. I had little choice but to place the knife against the zombie's throat, just above my hand and start sawing.

It took a little time, but I finally got the knife to the spine and severed the cord. The second my blade touched the spinal cord, the zombie dropped to the ground. Its head was still deadly, and I was careful as I let go of the gooey throat. Reversing my grip on the blade, I spiked it down and it easily pierced the skull, killing the zombie for good.

CHAPTER 28

I stood up, and was about to berate my companions when I saw they were having some trouble of their own. The zombies on the stairs had finally reached the top and had managed to come up to us from behind. Jake was standing on a bench, methodically cracking zombie skulls with what looked like a bored expression on his face.

Julia was spinning her staff, alternately killing with her blade or the metal ball on the other end. She would hack on their necks with the big blade, more often than not killing her attackers, or she would use the ball to crack a head or two.

Julia had one zombie left, and it was a big one. This guy must have been six foot five and he came charging at the little woman. Julia took one look at him and suddenly jumped into the air, bringing the ball down as hard as she could on his crusty head. The metal ball landed with a crunch, and the undead giant toppled forward without a sound.

Jake was fairly indiscriminate when it came to his killing. He didn't think anything about it, he did not even see the zombies as little more than an annoyance. It always got to me how cool Jake was able to stay in the face of danger. At least, he was according to what Jake had said. Jake was playing a kind of game, which he cheerfully described as death by gravity. He wouldn't kill them when he smacked them, he preferred to hit them in the shoulder and knock them over the side of the railing. Each one that he hit made a squishing sound that really sounded disgusting. I was glad we weren't able to see over the side into the gloom.

Jake smacked the last one on his side, and it slammed against the railing, but it didn't go over. Julia kindly provided assistance in the form of a push with her metal ball, and the zombie went over obligingly.

Jake looked at me. "How's the exit looking?

"As good as can be expected. I haven't had a chance to look, so I'll head over there now.

"Mind yourself," Jake said, pausing to grab a golf towel from the store to wipe off his mace.

"No worries this time," I said. "I think all of the activity is concentrated at the end with the zombies looking out." I thought for a second. "I just hope there's not too many of them, since I am running out of ideas."

"We got your back," Jake said, winking a Julia.

I grinned and went back to where I had first encountered my gruesome friend. I took the corner wide this time, not looking for any errant behavior, I just wanted to get out of this crazy place. I was starting to wonder if we were ever going to get out of this place.

One look down the hallway and I knew it wasn't going to happen. Not unless we decided to open up with our guns. If there was one zombie down there, then there was at least thirty. And the ones closest to me, which were about twenty feet away, slowly turned and started their inevitable shuffle in my direction.

I looked back at Jake and Julia. "Moving on," was all I said.

Julia and Jake cleared the corner and then hurried to catch up. We normally didn't use our guns unless we absolutely had to, and then it was not something we did on a routine basis. Ammo was plentiful for us, but we had been trained for so long in gun-less fighting that it didn't make sense to start shooting now. Besides, Jake and I weren't the greatest shots. Dad used to kid us, telling us the safest place to be when we opened fire was to be near the target. He had room to talk, being able to zap a zombie at fifty yards with a pistol, six hundred with a rifle.

We moved into Macy's and immediately we were sweating. There were dozens of places for a zombie to hide, so many corners that I was nervous as hell. I tried to steer wide of most of them, but there were so many it was almost a wasted effort. I took to holding my axe out in front of me, figuring that a zombie might grab it first, giving me some kind of warning before it attacked. It didn't help that it was really dark in the store, with glow coming from the back that caused freaky shadows.

Jake sidled up next to me. "Can't say this is an improvement, brother," he said as he peered over a cosmetics counter. "What's this stuff?"

Julia glanced over. "Mom said it was for looking pretty. You want to look pretty?"

Jake shrugged. "Thought already I did."

I moved away, since there was nothing I could add to that conversation. At the center of the store, there were some funny-looking stairs that led to a black hole. I couldn't see anything past the first fifteen stairs and it was all blackness.

I looked at Jake and he just shook his head. "No goddamn way. Uh, uh."

Julia peered in and suddenly she sucked in her breath. "Oh God."

I looked down and saw what had to be a hundred pair of glowing eyes staring up at us, several moving towards the stairs and a couple already on the way up.

Suddenly, I was mad. I had been chased from one end of this mall to the other, with literally nothing to show for it. Down in that pit was a mess I could do something about, and do it right now.

I pointed towards the door. "Get over there and make sure nothing gets in my way."

"What are you going to do?" Jake asked. "Come on. Let's all just get the hell out of here."

"Aaron, what are you going to do?" Julia tugged at my arm. "Let's get out of here, come on!"

"Cover the door," I said, drawing my sword. "I'll be there in a minute. Trust me."

"Aaron, you're fucking nuts! You can't go down there!" Jake was nearly frantic as the first zombies were just a few steps away."

"Move it!" I snarled at the two of them. They both looked at me as if I was about to commit suicide, and I can't blame them, considering what I must have looked like.

They ran to the door, and stood inside the foyer, keeping a barrier between themselves and any surprises that might be wandering around. I could see Julia biting her lip as she does when she's nervous. I would have winked if I thought she could see me, but it was too dark where I was.

The first zombie reached the top of the stairs and I promptly kicked it in the chest, crashing it into the one behind it and causing a domino effect on the stairs. In just a few seconds, I had managed to halt the progress on the stairs. The zombies struggled to regain their footing, and the ones pushing from behind didn't help the ones trying to get to their feet on an uneven surface. Many of the zombies fell down again, and some of them didn't get back up.

I didn't wait to see if they'd make it to the top again. I knew there were other zombies in this place and causing a ruckus here would just attract them. So I went over to a rack that had a lot of strange pieces of clothing. Long strips of brightly colored cloth in various patterns and shapes. They tapered from one end to the other and had little points on either end. I could not imagine what the heck they were for, but it didn't matter because they were perfect for what I had in mind.

I took out my small bottle of kerosene and squirted a good amount over the fat ends of the strips. Taking the small ends in my right hand while my left flicked as lighter, I made a blazing torch in a couple of seconds. The store was lit up from one end to the other from the flames and a quick glance around showed me I wasn't alone and would have company very soon.

I swung the strips wide and flung the flaming brands out over the black hole, and the orange flames illuminated the walls as they floated down. The fifteen or so strips landed on the head and shoulders of several zombies, and I could see our original estimate was way off. There had to be at least two hundred of the nasty things down there in the basement.

The flames caught the clothing and hair of the zombies they touched, and set off additional fires. In a short while, there was a lot of fire coming out of the pit, and we were in serious danger of suffocating if we weren't able to get out.

One zombie from the main floor came at me and I used my blade to hack off the heads of a couple more zombies that clearly needed a lesson in physics. The meeting between flesh and sharpened steel always favored the steel. I walked away from the burning pit, and I was happy to see that the walls were catching fire. This place would be free of zombies if the whole thing went up. As it was, I would be happy if that pit of gross was eliminated.

Another zombie was clawing at the glass that separated it from my brother and Julia, and a second was working its way around a perfume counter to join the fun. I waited a second for the perfumed one to get closer; a female wearing what looked to be a very decayed fur coat. Her hair was completely gone, but for some reason her lipstick was perfect. Go figure. I backhanded her with the sword in the neck and watched her bald head bounce away and into a rack of pants. She managed to get a bite into the pants and swung there like a small dog hanging on a rope toy.

My activity caught the attention of the zombie at the glass, and it came at me faster than I thought it would. It was a teenager, which meant it was going to be faster than your normal zombie was. I didn't have enough time to do anything other than bring my blade to bear and the stupid dead thing impaled itself on my sword.

Stuck, its arms flung around in an attempt to grab me. I used the sword like a throwing stick and flung the zombie away from me. It slammed into the glass, causing a crack near the floor. The zombie got up, but this time I was ready, and in the mood to show off a little.

The kid came again and from the middle ready position, I thrust the blade forward and up, catching him in the chin and shoving the blade through his skull to where the point stuck out from the top of his head. He was dead instantly, but as I withdrew the blade, I swung quickly and managed to sever his head as he fell to the floor.

I wiped my blade off on his hoodie and stepped through the door, grateful for some air that wasn't filling with smoke. I coughed my hello to the two of them, and we all went out the door to the sunshine and fresh air. I had to remember to burn off any residue on my blade, so I didn't sheath it.

Julia looked at me like I was crazy, and Jake just stood there watching the smoke fill the store, while burning silhouettes stumbled around causing more fires.

"Aaron?" Jake asked.

"Yes?"

"Nice work. That last kill was pretty cool."

"Thanks."

"Let's get the heck out of here."

I looked over at the horde of zombies that was hanging out by one of the entrances. They were the reason we had run into the mall in the first place. They had cut us off from out ride and we had nowhere else to go.

"Good plan." We ran over to the truck and hopped inside. I secured my big blade in the rear. I didn't want to put it in its sheath because any virus on it could transfer to the sheath, and I would just be putting it on the sword every time I sheathed it. God help me if I ever scratched myself or someone else and I thought that blade was clean.

We drove away from the mall, and we could see smoke rising from a hole in the roof. Maybe the rest would go, who knew. However, on the upside, we'd managed to kill quite a few zombies, which always favored the living

In the truck, we were silent. We hadn't yet picked up the object we had been hired for, and we'd already wasted a day. Not a good start. We'd spent the morning getting up to this point, and the noon hours running around a mall, evening was coming on and we were going to have to spend the night somewhere.

"Remind me why we were near that mall?" I asked. I had thought about it and couldn't come up with a decent answer.

"Julia's idea," Jake said, stealing a glance at our silent partner.

"I'm sorry! I just wanted to get some new clothes! Mine are getting faded, and we don't live near enough to a big community to find something for me." Julia pouted and crossed her arms.

"No harm done. We're just another day out. It's not like we had any pressing matters at home." I tried to play mediator, but I don't think it was going well.

"Fine. I'll just let my clothes fall off of me. Happy?" Julia threw that out there as a challenge.

I didn't expect myself to say anything, but I did. "I'd be happy."

Julia started slightly and stared at me for a second before locking her eyes on the road ahead. A slight pinkish color worked its way up her neck and settled on her cheeks.

Jake laughed. "Good lord! You're going to get yourself killed, Aaron. You must have learned your sense of humor from Uncle Duncan."

I didn't say anything, as that wasn't such a bad compliment, all things considered.

CHAPTER 29

We pulled into the capital just as the sun was going down. There was still a decent amount of activity, but a lot of people had been getting up at dawn and hitting the sack at dusk for so long it was a habit hard to break. Dad always joked that it took a zombie apocalypse to get a full night's sleep finally.

Jake and Julia delivered the collected items, this time it was a set of china and some strange glassware that I found out later was called Depression glass. It didn't make me feel any different, so I didn't understand that at all.

We met up back at the truck and Jake was in kind of a foul mood. I didn't want to get into it with him, so I asked him what was wrong.

"Nothing. Everything. I don't know." Jake was in rare form tonight.

I turned to Julia and she answered for Jake. "Jake informed the man who paid us that it wasn't a tough trip, and there wasn't any activity in the area at all. The man said he knew that, he just felt like having someone else go get his stuff for him. It was worth the money to *not* have to go, he said," Julia explained.

That made Jake's mood clearer. I knew he was looking for something, anything else, and this would contribute to the feeling. I didn't know what else to tell him.

"I'm sorry, Jake," I said.

That seemed to have an effect. "Not your fault, Aaron. It's just a sign of the times. Maybe this was the signal we needed to get out of this collection business and get into something more permanent. Something that actually makes a contribution to the country," Jake said, looking out over the river.

I shook my head. This was really out there, even for Jake. Everything I thought I knew about him was going sideways. Contribution? Not my brother. Permanent? Yeah, sure.

"Any ideas?" Truth be known, I was a little scared. I didn't know what else to do, and I didn't have any skills that would make any kind of contribution he was talking about.

"Not yet. But it's not like we don't' have time and we certainly don't need the money."

That was very true. With what we had from all of our collecting lately, and the money my father left me, we were very comfortable right where we were. If we were to move to town, we'd be one of the richest people here. The thought of it was kind of enticing.

"Tell you what. Let's get a drink to celebrate and we'll head home in the morning. We won't even look at messages for a week, just take a break and enjoy the summer days for a change," I said, hoping to sidetrack Jake's mental process and delay any action that might have me looking for another line of work.

Jake laughed. "Deal."

We walked together across the street, and down the hill towards the riverfront, where there were a number of establishments serving decent home-brewed beer and found liquor. People had been making the stuff for years, but a bottle of pre-zombie booze was a luxury several people were willing to pay big coin, even for a glass. Something to do with helping their memories or something.

As we were walking, the sun finally slipped behind the trees of the hills to the west, and the valley began to darken quickly. Many homes were dark, yet several had lights still on as people finished daily chores or did their reading. I knew this, because I had a bad habit of looking into house windows as I went past. I guess it was just my curious nature. Jake and Julia always said I was just nosey.

We went into a small place called The Letter after Z, which was some reference to the zombie wars. Jake knew the owner; he was a friend of our father's back in the old days when people were fighting for their lives on a daily basis.

The place was decently populated, and there was a fair mix of people inside. Several men at the bar looked like tradesmen, while a couple others looked like craftsmen. At a couple of tables in the corner, a group of merchants quietly argued over the price of something, and in another corner a very drunk man tried desperately to pick up a local prostitute and was failing miserably.

At another table, several rough-looking individuals were speaking in low tones, and they all turned to stare at Julia as we walked in. I thought a couple of them looked familiar, but I wasn't sure enough to bring it to the attention of the others.

We moved to the bar and ordered drinks, and Jake exchanged pleasantries with Jason, the owner. Jason had been with our father when they had struck out on their own and made it here, and had stayed ever since. Jason was probably approaching his fifties now, but his eyes were still as sharp as ever. He leaned close to Jake and whispered something quick, then went off to tend to another customer.

Jake leaned on the bar, his beer in one hand and the other near his belt. Julia smiled warmly as she worked on her glass of wine, and snuggled in between Jake and myself. I looked over her head at my brother, who looked at Julia and then shrugged at me.

Worked on my own beer and let my thoughts drift. I was still wondering what I might do if I wasn't collecting anymore and I tried to come up with some possibilities. I was still only twenty-one, so I had a lot of time to figure things out.

In the middle of my thoughts, some low voices reached me, and I realized that I was overhearing parts of the conversation at the corner table.

"That's the guy that faced off Casey not too long ago..."

"Big fella has some shoulders on him..."

"...but that's almost too fine an ass to waste on the boss."

"Forget the ass, did you check out her..."

"How you want to play it?"

"Let them drink, then we'll take them."

I was fully alert at this point and wasn't too sure what to do. I was getting angry, and knew Jake would probably lose it and kill someone, and we'd all be in trouble if he did that. I decided to let it go and see where they wanted to take this. Just to be on the safe side, though, I did unsnap the holster at my belt and on the knife at my waist.

I drank a little more when I felt a touch on my shoulder. I looked over and down into Julia's very blue eyes.

"Hi," She said.

"Hey." I replied.

"What's on your mind?"

"Just wondering if I was going to have another," I lied.

Julia smiled very sweetly, and then got up on her tiptoes to whisper in my ear.

"Bullshit. Why are you getting your weapons ready?"

I smiled back and leaned over to whisper in her ear. I told her about what I had overheard, and when I finished, I gave her a kiss on the cheek to complete the ruse that we were a couple sharing an intimate moment.

Julia smiled and put a small hand on her cheek, then put another one on the small of my back. On the surface, it was an affectionate gesture, but the hilt of one of my knives was back there and she'd be able to get it out faster than her own weapon.

Jake looked over at me and cocked an eyebrow at Julia's intimacy, but got serious when I winked at him and flashed my teeth. It was a signal we had worked out years ago in case we ever ran into trouble involving living people. On the surface, it looked like we were sharing an inside joke, but he knew something was up.

We didn't have long to wait. Jake decided to go to the bathroom, leaving an open space next to Julia. One of the men got up from the table and walked over, leaning on the bar and facing Julia and myself. He was a big man, easily my size, but with a much bigger gut. The fat didn't fool me, though. He had heavy arms, and his forearms were corded with muscle. This was a guy, who could not only take punishment, but could also dish it out with equal enthusiasm.

"Hey, little lady, you from around here?" The man asked while signaling Jason for service.

Julia didn't even glance at the man, she just ducked under my arm, coming up underneath my chin and leaning back into me. She ran a hand up and down my arm, and I was almost surprised enough to forget it was an act.

The man seemed put out. "Huh. Some fuckers have all the luck." The man looked me up and down, and then ordered a round of drinks for his table. While he waited, he leaned over and stared hard at Julia, trying to look down her shirt and sizing her up like a piece of meat. If she were my woman, I'd have cut his throat for his insulting gaze. As it was, we were just pretending to keep up the notion we were oblivious.

Julia wasn't helping at all. She brought her hands up, stretching as she did so, and put her hands behind my neck, turning her head into my chest and humming contentedly. She wiggled her butt against my legs, and it was hard to remember where the hell I was, let alone what I was doing there.

Big man got his drinks and walked back to the table, sitting heavily and muttering to his friends. "Ain't nothing. Won't even face a challenge in his face."

"Largo will pay a lot for the hot blonde, I guarantee it. Least forty silver."

"You think? He's never paid that much before..."

I didn't hear the rest, because Julia had turned around, and had slipped her hands in between my vest and my shirt, stroking my sides and back.

I swallowed before I spoke. "I think they're planning a jump after we leave. You can come out from there."

Julia looked up at me and smiled slightly. "I like where I am, Aaron." She hugged me tightly, resting her head on my chest. "I feel safe with you."

I was stunned. Julia had never expressed any kind of feeling for me before, even with all we had been through. I always thought she had feelings for Jake, seeing as she knew him longer and was closer to his age. I didn't know what to do, so I brought my arms together around her and hugged her back. Julia sighed and melted against me, and I suddenly felt better than I had for months.

CHAPTER 30

"Get a damn room!" A harsh voice barked across the room and I turned slightly to see it came from the table with the troublemakers.

I turned back to holding Julia, and the voice came again. "Shit, boy, you want a piece of that ass? Crack it open so we all can have a turn!"

Rough laughter broke out from the table and the entire bar went silent. Jason looked hard at the men at the table, but he wasn't in a position to interfere. Jake was nowhere to be seen, and I had Julia to worry about.

I don't know why I decided to push the issue. I guess I really was my father's son. I pulled away from Julia and turned towards the men at the table. They were still laughing, but they were a little more cautious, as I was still large, and still well armed.

I walked up to the table and stopped at the edge. The men looked me up and down with contempt, and the one who had originally went up to the bar spoke first. "Tell you what, boy, I'll be generous. I'll give you a copper a screw, and you can keep the change!"

The rest of the bar took a breath. That wasn't even the rate for the worst of whores and to suggest giving change for a copper was enough to get you killed in most parts of the country these days. No jury would convict you for dealing with the insult.

I chuckled slightly, and shook my head. I put two hands on the table and shoved downward, the far edge lifted up and when it was even with a very surprised big man's mouth, I shoved it forward, jamming it into his face and removing a couple of his teeth. I didn't stop there. As the two men closest to me stood up, I swung my fists outwards, smacking both men in the nose and dropping them to the floor. I grabbed the edge of the table and twisted it sideways, knocking it into a fourth man, and spilling the two of them to the floor. The final man charged from the side, but went down in a heap when I kicked him in the crotch.

In a matter of seconds, I had cleaned out the table and men were slowly picking themselves up off the floor, several leaving blood behind from busted noses and teeth. I stepped back to see if anyone wanted any more, when I stopped dead.

Something cold was pressed against my neck, just below my ear, and it didn't take much imagination to realize someone was jamming a gun against me. I put my hands up about chest high and held them out slightly from me.

"Nice moves, boy, but knowing who your father was, I'm not surprised. Before you think you're fast enough to take me, understand I've been killing zombies and men years before you were born, and I know how to kill." The voice sounded old and raspy, like someone who had been gargling with gravel every morning for twenty years.

"Now then, let's talk about what you've done here. You've interrupted my business, and whetted my appetite for some *different* business, so how might we work this out?" The voice came from about my shoulder, so I figured that if he had his arm fully extended, I could get him if moved right. But I had to get it perfect the first time.

"Motherfucker! I'll kill you for this!" The big guy I had hit in the face with the table rushed forward and I couldn't do anything as he brought his fist back and slammed it into my gut. I tried to tense against it, but I still wound up doubling over. I recovered quickly enough, only to find the gun pressed against my head again.

"Aaron!" Julia started forward, but stopped when the voice spoke again.

"Stay there, missy. You'll be coming with us soon enough, don't worry. Your boyfriend is getting a lesson, that's all." The man cackled and I felt the cold fire building in me again. I closed my eyes, and when I opened them, the man who hit me took a step back. He recovered quickly enough and this time he shifted his aim, looking to land a punch square in my face.

It never made it. When his fist was past my hand, I slapped his wrist, driving the punch away from me and into the arm that held the gun. I spun and grabbed the wrist holding the gun and pressed the elbow with my free hand, shoving the old man across the floor and crushing him face first into the bar. I didn't follow up right away, as I had a score to settle with the big man. He punched at me again, and I took the blow on the shoulder, bringing up a fist that started at my knees and ended on his chin. The sound was like a rock hitting a log, and the man's head snapped back from the impact. He took a step back, and then fell forward on his face. I didn't think we'd have any more trouble from him.

I walked over to the bar where the old man was trying to get up. He still held his gun, a small, stainless semi-automatic, but it hung loosely at his side. His other hand gripped the bar and he was using it to pull himself upright.

I didn't waste time, I grabbed the man by the collar of his shirt and hauled him upright, giving him a brutal punch to his kidney that elicited a short scream. The gun went off reflexively, and the bullet buried itself harmlessly in the old wood floor. I twisted his arm until he dropped the gun, and then spun him around to face me. He was a tough old piece of jerky, with black eyes and snow-white hair. Even in the face of certain doom, he was defiant. The sneer never left his face as I described what I was going to do to him and his men if I ever saw them again.

I was just finishing when I saw his eyes narrow, and then Julia screamed out.

"Aaron! Look out!"

I jerked to the side, and turned around, seeing the old man's men charging from the first scene of violence. I nearly jumped over the bar to put something between us when a dozen shots rang out, driving all of the men wounded to the floor.

The bullet holes were all in their legs and they bled everywhere. A single voice cried out from the outside of the bar. "Aaron, Julia! Let's get the hell out of here!

It was Jake. Apparently, in the middle of all the fun, he had decided to climb out the bathroom window and cover us from the rear.

I still held the old man, who made the mistake of opening his big mouth again.

"We'll meet again, boy. I look forward to screwing your girlfriend in front of you." He cackled again and ran a wet tongue over thin lips.

I slammed my fist into his chest, and watched his eyes bug out as he tried to take a breath. I squeezed his neck as I brought his face close to mine.

"That was just about half of what I can do. I just want you to know that next time I see you, I *can* and *will* rip your heart out." I threw the old man into the corner where he held his chest and neck. I picked up his gun and walked around the bleeding mess of toughs on the floor. Jake must have emptied the clip at the men, for everyone was shot at least twice.

Outside, Julia was waiting with Jake, and together we jogged away from the scene. We didn't need to answer any uncomfortable questions, and we didn't want to be delayed while the old man with the white hair called for reinforcements. Thus far, we hadn't need to kill anyone, but I had a feeling it was coming.

CHAPTER 31

We ran for a few blocks, and then walked slowly the rest of the way. Not anyone watching us would think we were running from anything, just out taking a stroll, and wouldn't pay much attention to us.

At the truck, Jake remembered he wanted to get some supplies from the store, so we drove to the edge of town and stopped at the indoor market. This was the place where merchants that were more affluent displayed their wares, being able to keep the weather off of them. Prices soared in the winter, but not so much that they lost business.

I asked Jake what we needed, and he told me to mind my own business. He'd said it would take just a minute. I wasn't in the mood to argue. I was tired and emotionally confused. All I wanted to do was go home, and unfortunately, that was a two-hour drive away.

Julia and I sat in silence for a few minutes. I was still processing what had happened at the bar when she leaned against me and took my hand.

"I wasn't acting at the bar, Aaron. I do feel safe with you."

"I'm glad, Julia. I'd hate to think we'd been in as many situations as we have and you thought I was useless." I had no experience talking to women. Growing up where I did, I had my mom, my aunts, and Julia, who up until now, always gave the impression that I wasn't measuring up. Suddenly, I was safe, and it was very confusing.

Julia processed that for a second, and then shifted herself. In an interesting maneuver that required a move forward, then up, then sideways, she was suddenly sitting in my lap, locking her hands behind my neck. Unbidden, my hands went around her waist, as if it was the most natural thing to do.

"I know I've been a shit sometimes, but I was always worried about the chances you take. Sorry," Julia said, looking down.

"It's okay. Nice to know you care," I replied.

"Thank you for sticking up for me back there," Julia said, changing the subject. She leaned in and placed her head on my shoulder. Her gentle breath on my neck was causing the truck to feel very warm all of a sudden.

"I was saving lives," I said. "If I let you at them, they'd have been killed."

Julia laughed and settled in a bit more, and without thinking, I turned my head and kissed her on the forehead. She responded by turning up her face and looking me in the eyes. I moved my head down and kissed her mouth, gently, hoping I wouldn't be rejected.

Julia responded in kind, her lips slightly parted to meet mine. We kissed for a long time, just taking in each other's breath, not wanting to do anything more than savor the moment. It was my first real kiss with Julia, and one that I would remember forever.

Right up to the point where Jake opened the driver door and said, "Jesus. I leave you two for five minutes and you're practically eating each other. What the hell?"

Julia and I broke our kiss and she slid off my lap to take her spot on the bench seat between us. She still held my hand, and managed to elbow Jake as he settled in to drive.

"Ouch. Well, do you want the good news or the bad news?" Jake asked.

"The bad." I knew Jake met with a merchant who was his contact for various collecting jobs. Typically, the jobs that no one else could do we were given, and we did that because they paid so well. Sometimes we collected stuff for merchants, turning it over for a percentage of the sales. Rare stuff that no one else had access to paid really well, especially if another merchant wanted it.

"Guy wants us to do a job in Joslin," Jake said.

"Dear God, I hope you said no," I said, shocked. Joslin was a killing ground, more so than Chicago was. Dozens of collectors had gone in there over the years and barely a handful had made it out. Joslin was legendary for its zombies, and very few people knew why. The zombies were said to be...not like zombies. They were faster, smarter, stronger; you name it. It was a bad place, and no one went there without a hugely good reason.

Jake smiled. "I said yes, and that's what brings us to the good news. The pay will be two hundred gold pieces, a quarter of which I got in advance." Jake held up a money tube, and sure enough, there was a pile of gold coin in there.

I had nothing to say. It was more money than I had seen in my life, outside of what my father had left me. We would be so well established we could stop working for five years and never want for anything. Maybe that was why Jake was willing to risk our necks for this little adventure. It was to give us some thinking room to figure out what we wanted to do with our lives. Or in my case, what I was supposed to do with my life.

"What are we going after?" Julia asked. I was curious about that, myself. What would merchants want so badly that they would be willing to spend a huge amount of money to obtain? What kind of potential profit would they see from it that made the bill worthwhile?

"I wasn't told what it was, exactly," Jake said, uneasily. "I was given very specific instructions to a very specific place, and told to take a very specific item."

"That's it?" I was extremely suspicious. After what we had just gone through, I didn't put it past the man in the white hair to have an ambush set up and we would be walking merrily right into it, dreaming of spending money instead of paying attention.

"That's it. Something called a 'server', whatever the hell that is. The guy started talking to me about the internet, but I really wasn't paying attention." Jake shrugged as he started the truck and we pulled away. We were still avoiding trouble from Jake's firearms show, and we needed to be gone.

"Well, if you're sure, then I guess it's a go. After this, though, we need to stop for a while, anyway. I need to straighten things out about what I'm going to be doing and where I'm going to be headed with my life," I said. Julia squeezed my hand but didn't offer any help.

We drove west, then south. The big highways around here were clear, save for a few errant travelers, and we made decent time. About an hour after we started, we were in the town of Mayfair, and Jake announced he was too tired to go on and we should spend the night in the lovely community of Mayfair. I wasn't about to argue, as I was dead tired and couldn't keep my eyes open much longer. Julia had already nodded off once or twice, snapping awake when her head slumped onto her chest.

Jake pulled into the town and found a small farmhouse out at the edge. It was unoccupied, and we stepped in carefully, checking the rooms for any unwanted guests. The house was sparsely furnished, with just the essentials in place for short visits. I didn't bother arguing about the master suite, I simply took my gear off and stretched out onto the floor. Jake wasn't so indiscriminating, announcing that he was going to have the master bedroom. Julia settled for one of the other rooms upstairs, and I have to admit her leaving me by myself put me off a little. I began to wonder if the truck episode had anything to do with anything, or if I was just being nuts.

I told myself it didn't matter and I just stretched out on the floor and went to sleep. I doubt it took me more than five minutes to slip into slumber, that's how tired I was.

CHAPTER 32

In the middle of the night, I awoke to a strange sound. It seemed like there was something sliding slowly around the house. It was a soft sound, as if someone was gently touching the walls as they walked around. The room I was sleeping in was pitch black, save for a thin strip of moonlight coming in from outside. If I remembered correctly, Dad used to call this Rustler's Moon. It was too dark to get a bead on anyone who was stealing the cows, yet it was light enough to avoid pitfalls as you went in to steal other people's cattle.

After a couple more minutes of scratching, I heard nothing, so I went back to sleep, deciding it must have been the wind or something. I didn't know much about old houses, but I suspected they creaked and groaned a lot, just like the lodge did from time to time.

I went back to sleep, and figured I would be able to get to morning without any more interruptions.

What seemed like a long time later, I woke suddenly to a small hand on my chest. I looked up and saw that Julia had come down and was lying next to me, her hand on me. Her leg was thrown across my legs, and she was wearing a simple t-shirt and what mom used to call "running shorts." I shifted my arms and managed to wrap her up and keep her from leaving. She used my left arm as a pillow and we both went back to sleep, comforted by the feeling of the other. It was a strange, sweet, wonderful feeling.

I awoke in the dark hours of the morning, when the sun hasn't yet turned the sky to grey, but was working on it. I had no reason to wake up, but something pulled me awake. Julia had turned herself in the night and was still using my arm as a pillow, but had her back to me. I rolled to the side and wrapped my free arm around her. She sighed and scooted back into me, and we lay there for a while. I will admit my thoughts were all over the place and many of them were not to be repeated in polite company.

I heard a step outside and something hit the house. It wasn't a hard hit, but I was instantly awake. Julia felt me tense and turned her head.

"What is it?" She asked, bringing her right arm up to stroke my neck.

"Something's outside," I said, getting up on one elbow.

"Probably a dog. " She shifted onto her back, which put her directly beneath me and she still lay on my forearm. Julia pulled me down for a kiss, which I wasn't about to refuse, even though there might be a horde of zombies outside.

We kissed for a while, and might have done more, when the noise repeated itself. I disengaged from Julia and got to my hands and knees. "No dog does that twice. Better get upstairs and dressed, we might have to move fast," I said.

Julia pouted, but knew better than to argue. Of the three of us, I had the best instincts for trouble. Jake just plowed into it, Julia dealt with it, but I had a way of knowing it was coming. I had that feeling right now.

I stayed on the floor, and got myself ready. I didn't want to be seen from the windows, and hoped Jake and Julia wouldn't make too much noise coming down. I put my gear on, and crawled over to a window on the side of the house I thought I heard the noises coming form. I stood up slowly by the window, keeping myself out of sight. The good news was that no one on the outside would be able to see in very well unless we did something stupid like turn on a light. The bad news was we couldn't see very well outside either.

I leaned against the wall and slowly brought my head away. I could see outside, and in the graying dawn, there was definitely something in the yard. I couldn't tell exactly what it was, but it was something, and it was moving slowly.

I backed away from the window and stayed low. I moved slowly as to keep from attracting attention. My gut told me there was a zombie in the yard, and my instinct told me there was more than one. I moved silently towards the stairs and spent a few anxious moments trying to get up the wooden steps without too much creaking. At the top landing, I ran into Julia, who was much more dressed than she was before.

"Hey, you." She smiled at me and gave me a hug. "Everything okay?"

"Right here, yes. Outside, no," I said, pulling away. "There's a zombie in the yard, and I have a feeling there's more than one." I went over to Jake's door and tapped softly. I hoped he was already up, but I didn't put much faith in that. I opened the door and saw he was still sleeping. I couldn't wake him like I wanted to, by pouring a bucket of cold water on his head. I had to settle for subtle.

"Jakey? Time to wake up. Jaaakey..." I tried to sound like our mother had when we were younger. For whatever reason, she never had to raise her voice. We would jump up at that sound as if we had been caught doing something we shouldn't have.

Jake cracked an eye at me, and then tilted his whole head my way. "Aaron? What gives?" Why are you up here?"

"Zombie in the yard. Might be more. Better get dressed." I kept it simple for the morning hours. Anything longer was a waste of time.

Ten minutes later, we were at the top of the stairs. It was the one place in the house we couldn't be seen from any windows, and being centrally located, our voices wouldn't carry as far.

"I only saw the one, but I get the feeling there's more," I said.

"Any proof of that?" Jake asked, looking at his magazines and loosening his knives.

"None outside of gut feeling," I replied, taking out my tomahawk and checking the edges.

"Good enough for me," Jake said. "What do you want to do?"

Julia spoke up. "It's stupid to just go out there when it's dark. The sun is coming up. Why not wait until we can see and then go deal with it, or them?"

"Sounds good to me," I said. "I just wish we hadn't parked the truck so far away and left all of our heavy guns in it, along with our spare ammo."

"Stop being so damn gloomy," Jake admonished. "We're in Mayfair. Population of about a hundred. They all came here from other places, and all are survivors. If this sucker wanders their way, it'll be dead before it knows it. Besides, what's one zombie to us, anyway?"

I had to admit he had a point, so I sat down on the top of the stairs and lay back onto the floor. Julia sat down with her back to the railing post so we could talk, albeit quietly. Jake went back to his room and stretched out on the floor, trying to get a few more winks before it became too difficult to sleep.

Julia and I spoke of nothing, and everything. A nice conversation didn't have to do with anything we did for a living. We talked about our mothers, our fathers, and about what we wanted to do with this life. Julia managed to put into words something I had been feeling, but couldn't quite wrap my words around.

"I feel like our dads left us a world that had a pretty good start, but somewhere along the way, things got a little confused, and if something isn't done, we're not going to like what the world will become. I mean, they founded a new country, but it seems like it's falling backwards, and not going forwards. Like we're wasting our potential and it will take generations to recover, if we ever do," Julia said.

I nodded in agreement. "It's like the virus that makes the zombies. It starts out small, like a bite, but it spreads and kills and creates something unrecognizable from the original."

"Exactly. Question is, what is it and what do we do about it?" Julia looked at me with her very blue eyes and I wondered if my dad ever felt weak like this when mom looked at him the same way. It was strange, but it kind of gave me a purpose. I felt like I needed to do something to make this world a better place for Julia.

"Not sure entirely for the future, but for right now, we need to get home, get this job done, and then we can focus on what to do about the backward decline we're seeing," I said, locking my hands behind my head and closing my eyes. Julia lay across me, with her head on her hands, looking at my face. I kept my eyes closed, just enjoying the moment. I didn't know what the future held, but I was starting to get an idea and it wasn't half bad.

CHAPTER 33

An hour later, I shook Julia and we both got up. It was much lighter outside and we could see a whole lot more, so we went into the room where Jake was and found him at the window looking out.

"Any sign of our friend?" I asked.

"Which one?" Jake replied ominously.

"What do you mean?" Julia asked.

Jake pulled away from the window with a shake of his head. "Didn't see this coming."

I looked outside and my stomach did a turn. There had to be twenty zombies outside and those were just the ones I could see.

"Where in hell did these guys come from?" I asked rhetorically.

"No idea," Jake said. "Maybe they had an outbreak at Mayfair and the lights of the truck brought them over here last night. Not finding anything, they've just hung out here before something causes them to move."

"Can we get them to move?" I asked. I knew it was an impossible question, but you never knew. "Unless you have a cat or dog in your pocket that needs to be somewhere else in a hurry, I'd say we're pretty much screwed if they figure out we're in here," Jake replied.

"I can't tell you how grateful I am we left our heavy weapons in the truck," I said, looking down on the scene. About fifteen to twenty zombies milled about aimlessly, while in the distance, more were coming. Just outside our vision, it looked like there were zombies on the ground, hunched over something. I really didn't want to know what it was, but I had a sneaking suspicion about what it could be.

"All right. So what do we have on us?" Julia brought us back into focus. "I have my gun, thirty rounds in my mags, and my knives. Aaron?"

"I've got my axe, two knives, my gun, and forty-five rounds on me." I said.

"All right. That's better. Jake?"

"Just my knives," Jake said.

"No gun?"

"In the truck."

"Ah. Okay, so we have seventy-five rounds between us, and knives and an axe. Anything else?" Julia asked.

We turned out our pockets and discovered we had a box of matches, a length of cord, a compass, and a toothbrush.

"Matches. This gives me an idea," Jake said. "This house will go up like a candle, and if we can get the ghouls inside, we can take a good number of them out without a shot."

"I know there's a catch," I said.

"Of course, there is, baby brother, but let me lead on this and educate you." Jake smiled and I casually tried to hit him, but he easily ducked my punch.

Jake educated the two of us. "I'm going downstairs and get into the basement to see what I can set on fire. I'll attract the attention of the zombies outside, and get them to come in for a treat. Hopefully by that time, the floor will be ready to go up and we can get the most burn for our buck."

"How will we get away without being incinerated?" Julia asked, voicing my own question and hers at the same time.

"We tie the sheets together to use as a rope, and head out a window with the least amount of zombies waiting for us." Jake acted as if he thought this was a silly question.

"And if you get delayed, or the zombies discover you before you can get back to us?" I asked.

"Then I might need some help," Jake said, clearly uncomfortable with the question.

"Tell you what, big brother. I'll go with you and wait at the stairs. At the very least, I can keep them off your back while you run for your life," I said, checking my gun. It was a stainless Beretta 92FS, at least that's what it said on the side. My dad gave it to me when I was sixteen, telling me it used to be my uncle's gun. It was the only thing I had of the man.

"Oh, that's kind of you. Thanks," Jake said. He was trying to be sarcastic, but it wasn't working through the relief he was obviously feeling.

"Just get moving. I want to get out of here as soon as I can," I said. I looked over at Julia. "You got the sheets part?" I asked.

Julia smiled. "I got it. And I'll cover your butts in case you need help from the stairway."

"Be right back." I followed Jake and we made our way carefully down the stairs. The stairwell led to the living room, and it was a short trip through the kitchen to the basement stairwell. Trouble was, several windows just to our left looked out onto the porch, and there were at least six zombies on the porch, just milling about and looking confused. It was our first chance to get a good look at them. They were all fairly fresh, as far as zombies go, which meant Mayfair or somewhere close just had a bad outbreak. Their flesh hadn't turned white yet, and they looked pretty normal. A few had wounds, but the majority had no marks on them at all that we could see. For an outbreak, this one was surprisingly clean. Another thing that was odd was the number of ghouls that had ropes on their wrists. That made no sense at all.

Jake and I waited, looking for our chance to get away without being seen. It wasn't easy, since we also had to be careful of the windows in the kitchen. If a zombie happened to see Jake, it was over.

Quickly, Jake moved, and in a flash, he was gone. I heard him scramble through the kitchen, and then down the stairs. I had nothing to do but wait, and hope one of the zombies outside hadn't seen him. So far they weren't calling out, so we seemed to be lucky so far.

For what seemed to be an eternity, I waited on the stairs. I counted the pictures on the wall. I unloaded and reloaded all of my magazines. I figured out my axe was actually sharper than my knife. I tied and retied my shoes. I found myself bored enough that I was looking for a marker so I could put mustaches on the people in the pictures.

CHAPTER 34

Suddenly, Jake appeared and he was walking casually. He went into each room and waved to the zombies outside. He then went to the back door and opened it, waving and hollering at the zombies. In an instant, he was the most popular girl at the party, and everyone wanted to dance. When the drift started towards the door, he jogged back inside, and ran to the front door, hooting and making noise to get attention. When that worked really well, he bolted for the stairs and I was just a step ahead of him.

We waited at the top with Julia, who looked nervous and excited at the same time. She put her gun away, no longer needing it, and we waited for the house to start filling up. The first few zombies wandered through the downstairs, but not enough for what we wanted. The good news was zombies didn't look up all that often, unless they had a reason. If we stood still and became part of the furniture, we were relatively safe where we were. Of course, if we were downstairs, they would be ripping us to shreds right now.

The rooms began to fill up as more and more zombies came in the doors, and there were a good number of them at the bottom of the stairs. Smoke began to filter up as well, increasing out need to get out soon.

I took the opportunity we had to look at the zombies carefully. They were very fresh, having turned only a few hours ago. Considering how many there were, and the lack of injuries, there was something wrong about this setup. I was about to bring it up to Jake when he started yelling.

"Hey! Dumbasses! Up here, you ravenous wrecks! Come along, you can take a nice juicy bite out of my ass! Come on!" Jake was somewhat poetic in his smack-talk.

As one, dozens of heads turned upwards, and simultaneously they opened their mouths and groans. It wasn't a pretty sight, or a pretty sound. They all began moving towards the stairs, and the really creepy thing was they never broke eye contact. Even climbing the stairs, they would trip and fall, catch themselves or stumble down a bit, but they never stopped looking at us.

"Moving on," Jake said, and Julia pulled us towards the far bedroom. We left the other doors open, hoping we could fit as many as possible in the house before it completely went up.

Inside the room, we closed the door, and Julia stuffed a couple of pillowcases under the door right before Jake and I moved a heavy dresser in front of the door. It wouldn't hold them forever, but we just wanted to get them up here. The heavy footfalls in the hallway told us we were successful up to a point.

"When might we make our escape?" I asked, eyeing the sheets that were twisted together and tied to one leg of a brass-framed bed.

"We need to make sure as many of them are up here as possible." Julia wandered over to the door and screamed a few times. It sounded pretty realistic, like someone was losing their mind over the thought of being torn to shreds and eaten while still alive. Go figure.

Jake and I winced at the sound. "Didn't know she was an actress, too," Jake said.

I held my hands over my ears. "I'd have preferred not knowing."

Regardless of whether we liked it or not, it seemed to have the desired effect. Zombies began pounding on the door, and one of them managed to turn the knob, so the door began to open. Smoke poured into the room, and Jake and I had a hard time pushing back on the dresser. Our eyes were starting to water and it was getting hard to breathe.

"Time to go!" Jake said. I motioned for him to go and he shook his head at me. "Not this time, bro. You're heading out. Give me your gun, in case I need to buy some time."

I handed it over, and went to the window. Julia was waiting and I told her I would be going first, in case there was a problem   on   the   ground.
"You think I can't handle a zombie?" She challenged, with a little gleam in her eye.

"One, yes. Five, not so much. Remember the house in the city?" I reminded her of her hiding in a closet.

"Oh sure, you had to bring *that* up." Julia sounded down, but she handed over the sheet.

"This isn't getting easier!" Jake yelled from across the room.

"Gone!" I yelled back. I slipped out the window and slid down the rope of sheets. I tried to avoid the first floor window, and jumped the last six feet, pulling out my tomahawk and one of my knives. Julia was right behind me and landed heavily. She got up, and checked herself for injuries, finding none except to her pride. I knew better than to comment.

On the ground, there weren't any zombies nearby, but I thought I saw movement around the front. I looked up for Jake and watched him fly out of the window, trailing the sheets he held in both hands. The rope went taut, and Jake snapped around, slamming face first into the side of the house. He let go of the rope and fell the last five feet, landing on his back.

I wanted to go over and help him, I really did. But I couldn't do much more than stand there and silently shake from the laughter that kept me from moving to help. Julia was in no better shape, holding her hand over her mouth and facing away.

Jake didn't help the situation. He lay sprawled on the ground and made a noise like a cross between a moan and a burp. Every time he made the noise, I started laughing again.

After a few minutes, I was able to help, somewhat. I went over to Jake, and grabbed him by an arm. I dragged him away from the house, which was showing signs of a serious fire. I pulled him to his feet and he stood there holding his nose and his back.

"Heh, heh. Jake, heh, you okay? Hee hee." I tried to be serious, but it wasn't working. Julia was trying to hold it in, but air kept getting out and it sounded like her mouth was farting. That didn't help at all.

Jake leaned back, checked his hand for blood, and said, "Ow." He shook his head and twisted his torso. "Seemed like a good idea when I went over it in my mind."

"At least you didn't say 'Watch this,'" I said, returning to the land of the sane. "Come on, let's see if we need to finish off anyone." We went towards the front of the house, and through the windows, we could see flames were erupting out of the middle of the floor and up along the walls. The old wood in the building was perfect fuel for the fire, and it was spreading quickly.

Smoke was pouring out of the second floor windows, and anything living in there would have been dead a while ago. The dead things were still moving around, oblivious to the smoke and flames. On the first floor, several zombies had already caught fire, and were setting alight anything they bumped into. It looked like this was going to be quite the campfire in a few minutes.

In the front of the house, three zombies got up from their feast to come at us. I reached for my gun, only to realize Jake had it. I turned to Jake but he already had it out. He fired from the hip, and in three seconds, three shots rang out, and three zombies fell completely dead.

I was stunned. "What the hell was that? When we're on the range, you couldn't hit the side of a barn if you were standing inside it. You been holding out on us?"

Jake shrugged. "Can't explain it. If I take the time to aim, I nearly always miss. If I just snap a shot at something, I always hit it. It's like my brain turns off and lets my body do what needs to be done."

I shook my head. "Well, why not?" Julia just watched with a smirk on her face. "Gimme back my gun."

CHAPTER 35

We reached the spot where the zombies were and stopped cold. On the grass, there was a person, or rather what used to be a person. His hands were tied behind his back, and his mouth was gagged. He was wearing nothing more than a pair of underwear, and his legs, the parts that weren't chewed on, looked like they had been cut with something very sharp. His insides had been ripped out and eaten, and his face and throat were torn apart as well. His legs had huge strips of muscle torn away, and there was a lot of blood all over the place.

Jake looked the man over, then took his knife and used it to lever the man onto his stomach. The man's back was a mass of small wounds, and they looked like burns from where I was standing. As a precaution, Jake stabbed the man in the head, making sure he didn't come back later.

Stepping away, Jake looked at the ground then signaled Julia and I to get to the truck and follow. Curious, I did what I was told without protest.

Behind us, the flames had consumed the center of the house, and the rest was starting to go up. Two of the bedroom windows had opened up, allowing flames to escape in a rush towards the sky. It looked like we had managed to get all of the zombies inside, so I was calling that a victory, at least.

We followed Jake, who was studying the ground and walking slowly. It looked like he was tracking something, but I couldn't tell what it was. There weren't enough footprints to follow, and I didn't think Jake was a good tracker, so he had to be seeing something.

We followed Jake for about a mile, getting back into town. The trail led Jake to a playground by a school. I noticed as we drove that many houses had their front doors open, and several showed signs of violence, even from the street. The situation was very strange.

At the playground, there were a lot of rope pieces on the ground, and one door of the school was open. I stopped the truck and Julia volunteered to look inside, taking her melee weapon, just in case. I walked around the playground, wondering what Jake had seen and if he was seeing the same thing, I was.

I met up with Jake in the middle of the playground, and he was looking at something on the ground. I bent down and took a look, then stood up quickly. It was a large syringe, and inside was the blackest, vilest, most foul substance this side of hell could produce. It was a syringe full of Enillo Virus infected blood. That little needle had enough viruses in it to kill the entire population of the capitol without even breaking a sweat. It was half-full, and I began to understand where the other half went.

Jake looked at me, and his face was grim. "Here's how I see it. Someone, don't know who but I have an idea, came to this town last night and forced people out of their beds to come to this place. They were tied up and then injected with the virus from that syringe. One person was spared, and that person was wounded to the point that they bled profusely, making an easy trail for the zombies when they woke up. They followed the trail and were waiting for us when we stepped outside the home."

As much as I wanted to deny that scenario was too evil for someone to infect a town deliberately, the proof was right in front of me. "Who would do this and why?" I asked the obvious.

Jake sighed. "Not to be full of myself, but we were the targets. Who have we pissed of lately?"

I groaned. "Aw, damn. I should have killed that old man when I had my hand on his throat."

"How could you know? I have a feeling this was both an experiment, and revenge." Jake said.

Julia calling from the school interrupted us. "Jake! Aaron! Get in here!"

We ran with our weapons out, not knowing what to expect. We followed Julia through a couple of corridors, and ended up in a library. Spread out over the floor was about ten kids, varying in ages from a one year old to a twelve year old.

"Holy cow." I thought about what had happened, and I looked at a lot of very scared faces. The older kids were holding the younger kids, and several were sniffing as if they had been crying recently.

"They said men came in the night, and took them from their beds. They made them come here and took them from their parents. A man with a gun stood by the door, but he went away late last night. They didn't know what to do so they stayed here, waiting for their parents. They were going to go look for them when I found them," Julia said.

"Oh, boy," Jake said. "Well, they can't stay here. Let's see if we can round up some extra transportation and get them to either Ottawa or Morris."

We didn't have any worries about the kids. Someone would take them in. We were used to death, so when a parent passed away from either sickness or accident, everyone helped to find a place for any children.

I wasn't surprised the children had been spared. Since the coming of the zombies, and the settling of the country, children were highly valued. You could kill a man, take his stuff and burn down his house, and people might find a way to excuse it. But if you hurt a child, there was no place you would be safe. Every community would hunt you down and hang you. That is, if they bothered with a rope. You could easily just eat a bullet as well.

"I saw some vans on our way in, let's see if they work," Julia said.

"You stay with the kids; we'll be back in a minute," I said.

We found the vans, and even though only one worked, it was enough for the short trip. We packed up the kids and headed south. Julia drove the van, since the children seemed to trust her the most, and she would be the best person to relay the news about their parents.

Jake and I did some hard thinking, and it wasn't too far of a stretch to assume the trouble we had in the capitol was directly related to the trouble we had last night and this morning.

"What I can't get is the why? Why go to the trouble of rounding up a town, killing a man, and hoping that the zombies take care of your problem?" I asked rhetorically.

"No offense, little brother, but I think there was more to it than this, " Jake said.

"How so?"

"Someone who has taken the trouble to put together a team that will effectively take on a town, infect that town, and then guide the zombies to a target has put a lot of thought into this. I think we were a test case, and given who we are, no one would think twice about zombies killing us. It's a hazard of our chosen profession," Jake explained. "Eventually, the outbreak would have been reported, and the army would have come in and cleaned up, had we not taken care of the problem." Jake looked back to the huge plume of smoke rising in the morning sky, marking our recent activities.

"All right, but if it's a test, then what's the eventual end game? What are they hoping to do in the future? No one goes to this trouble and just uses it for nickel and dime stuff," I reasoned.

"Not sure about that. I don't think they planned on leaving the syringe behind, and someone probably caught hell for it. Maybe they plan on making a power move, who knows? Right now, I'm not inclined to care. If they want to take a piece of the country for themselves, go for it. There's enough to go around," Jake said.

"Doesn't work that way and you know it," I said darkly. "We weren't brought up that way."

"Yeah, well the guy who is supposed to be the country's moral compass bugged out, remember? All that talk about saving the country and restoring what we were is just a bunch of crap when the man himself decides to go on a selfish binge just because he lost his wife. So it's every man for himself, as far as I'm concerned," Jake said angrily.

"I'll remember you said that," I said.

"You do that."

"And his wife was your mother, biological or not. Grow up and deal with it," I replied.

Jake stared at me for a long time, and I returned his stare. This wasn't over, and I had a feeling someone was going to get seriously hurt when we finally settled up.

CHAPTER 36

We dropped the kids off in Ottawa, and told our tale to the local authorities. They promised to dispatch a team up to Mayfair and make sure there weren't any stray zombies wandering about. They were very disturbed to hear about the way things went down, and wanted to go to the capitol to complain. People began to talk about burning out the bad element, and it took the mayor of Ottawa a good half hour to calm everyone down.

After the grumbling died down, I told the assembled people that once we finished our last collection obligation, I was going to focus my attention on the problem at hand and make sure it didn't happen again, even if I had to hunt down the perpetrators myself and bring them to justice. I told them that if they went in a group, the bad guys might just go into hiding, and since they didn't know who they were hunting, it might all be for naught. Better to have two or three go, and get the job done without a huge uproar.

Jake glared at me the whole time I was speaking, and towards the end, turned away in disgust. Julia watched him go with an angry look on her face, and when she looked back at me, she was smiling.

I got a lot of nods of approval, and several people spoke in low tones to each other. One man spoke up as I was leaving.

"This really ain't your fight, Aaron. How come you're doing this?" He asked. A lot of people got quiet to hear my answer.

I thought for a second, and then gave the answer that come naturally to me.

"Because I can," I said simply.

It was really that easy. I didn't have a family, I didn't have a farm, or a real job that required my attention. I was well trained, experienced in going into bad places, and taught to find solutions to problems as they came up. I had an easy way with most people, and folks were inclined to trust me. It worked all around. The escapade at Mayfair was going to make the rounds, and the fact we brought the kids out was only going to help our standing with the locals.

Downside was the people who tried to kill us would know we survived, and may try very hard next time to finish the job.

Julia met with me and gave me a hug. "That was a nice thing to see. You actually sounded a lot like your father there for a minute."

I couldn't explain why, but that actually made me feel really good. "Thanks. Change in subject. What do you think pissed of Jake so much?"

Julia shrugged. "Short answer? Jealousy. Long answer? He's still trying to come to grips with the fact his real mother wasn't around, and his dad never explained it to him."

That made sense, although I couldn't figure out why he was holding it against me or why he would be jealous, and I said so.

"Take it up with him, he's a grump right now and I'm not talking to him," Julia said.

We walked back to the truck where Jake was waiting. Without a word, he climbed into the cab and started the truck. We rode all the way back to Starved Rock without speaking.

Jake parked the truck and went inside. I tried to stop him but his glare told me to either keep my mouth shut or arm myself. I decided to be quiet. Julia and I went out to the patio and spent the rest of the day just taking in the sun and enjoying each other's company.

The next day I expected to see Jake down at the meeting table with plans for the next collection. However, Jake was nowhere to be found. I looked in his room, down at the range, over by the Visitor Center, and even up at Eagle Point. All turned up empty. The vehicles were all there, so he had to be here somewhere.

I asked Julia if she had seen Jake, but she hadn't left the lodge all day, so she hadn't. It was becoming clear Jake was off doing something, and didn't want to be found. I could respect that, but we had a job to do, and I needed to figure out who was behind the attack on us the other day. I had my suspicions, and they centered on an old man with white hair and a bad attitude, but that was speculation and coincidence. Remarkable coincidence, to be sure, but I had no proof we were the target. For all I knew, the town was supposed to animate and go on a southerly rampage, but the one thing that cancelled that notion was the person they tortured to get to the house we were staying in. That made it personal. They were after us.

CHAPTER 37

On the second morning after our fight at the farmhouse, I went downstairs and found Jake sitting at the table. He was holding the memoir my father had left me and was finishing the last few pages. I was mad for an instant that Jake had read it before me, but I was calmed by the fact that Jake seemed to be in a much better mood. Maybe there was something in there he needed, and luckily found.

"How's the book?" I asked, breaking the silence.

Jake looked up. "Interesting. I never really believed Dad was able to do all the things people said he did. At least in here we have his word for it." Jake closed the book and slid it across the table to me. "This is going to sound strange, but I understand our father a lot better now, and I know what happened to my mother."

"Anything you want to talk about?" I asked.

"You can read about it, but in a nutshell, Dad had to make a lot of hard decisions, and he loved my mother very much. As much as he loved yours. I can see why it was painful for him to be here, and why he had to leave," Jake said.

I took all that in, and saw that Jake had come to some kind of peace, which was good for all involved.

"Want to talk about the next collection?" I asked.

Jake nodded. "Let's get Julia down here and we'll go over things. It should be a lot easier than I thought, mostly because the place we have to go is far outside Joslin proper, so the local zombie mess shouldn't be as much of a factor."

That was a relief. No one sane wandered into Joslin, and the only thing that we used from it was the power plant on the south side. Other than that, it was left to ruin. Zombies were there in force, and they were responsible for killing more than their fair share of collectors.

I had another question for Jake but he answered it before I got the chance to ask.

"About the other night, at Ottawa, I think you're right for wanting to go after the people responsible for Mayfair. We wanted to get out of collecting, and this would do it," Jake said.

You could have knocked me over with a twig. I really wanted to dive into that book now, but I could only ask one question. "Why?"

"Why the change? In all seriousness, Aaron, it's what we were supposed to do."

As soon as he said that, a weird feeling of relief washed over me. I'd been fighting the notion for a while, tying in our skills to a single purpose, which was to get stuff for people who couldn't, so they could have something from their former lives. But this was a new purpose, something we weren't collecting.

"No offense, Jake, but not so very long ago, you talked about being every man for himself, yourself included. Why the sudden shift?" I needed more than what he was giving me, and I didn't want to have to sift through the book to find it. Call me lazy, but this wasn't the Jake I knew.

"I'll put it like this, Aaron. Our dad wasn't content to just survive the zombie apocalypse. He spat in its face and dared it to come after him. He rebuilt the country for no other reason than you and me." Jake paused for a minute to let that sink in. "He lost countless friends, two wives, a mother, and a brother to this mess, but he kept it together.

"Let me ask you this, Aaron. Is the capitol a good place to be right now?" Jake looked over at Julia who had heard our voices and had come to the table.

"Not really," I said, thinking about the troubles that we have been having every time we go there.

"Wasn't always like that. Things have changed, and not for the better. We have it to do. We're expected to do it," Jake said.

Julia looked at me and I took her hand and gave it a squeeze. "Good thing you're not part of this guilt trip," I said.

Jake shook his head at Julia's nod. "Actually, she is. Her dad was as much a part of the rebuild as ours. There's some revelations in there for Julia as well. It comes down to this. Our dads fought a war, for us. We need to fight for the peace, for them. It's that simple."

We sat around the table looking at each other for a long time. I was at a loss for words, but I felt better than I had for months.

Julia broke the silence. "What are we supposed to do?"

Jake smiled that half smile of his and showed us a crude map of the place in Joslin we needed to go.

"We fulfill our obligation and then after that it's time to clean up."

CHAPTER 38

We spent the rest of the day getting things ready. This was going to be a trip up the road, and the good news was it wasn't going to be a long drive. Joslin was relatively close, and the place we had to get to, was on the west side, on the far edge of town. If we were lucky, it would be a quick in and out.

About noon, we finished our preps and had some time to kill. I sat down on the porch with Julia and together we started reading the book. It was nice to lounge on the patio with a gorgeous blonde in my lap, winding away the hours learning about our fathers.

We didn't get as far as I had hoped, since Julia insisted on making out every other chapter, but I wasn't complaining about the distraction. I had a healthy new respect for our fathers, and what they went through, trying to make the country again. When I read the part about Coal City, I suddenly realized how close I came to not existing at all. Julia discovered the truth about her parents, and was silent for a long time afterward. However, she handled it better than Jake did, realizing that her foster parents had done the best they could.

We all went to bed when the sunset, figuring to leave first thing in the morning. I stayed awake for a little while longer, reading and looking for clues as to where my father might have disappeared. I never thought for a second that he or Julia's dad might be dead. For whatever reason, I felt like I would know if he had passed, and I didn't get that feeling, ever.

The drive to Joslin was uneventful, each of us contributing to the conversation as to what we were going to do next. I played devil's advocate and wondered aloud why we were trained the way we were if our dads had made the world safe. Jake nailed that quickly by pointing out that we were probably the only ones that had been recently trained and who kept it sharp by using it all the time.

I couldn't argue that, so I tried a different tack. What would we do once we finished the new objective? Julia took that one, explaining that we probably would never be done, since we would have a lot of educating to do.

I took it at face value, and wondered to myself why I was questioning things so much. Part of me wanted very badly to believe that we were finally doing the right thing, that we would realize our true goal. The other part was intimidated by how big the goal actually was.

I kept those thoughts to myself as we turned off Route 6 and made our way through some very rough back roads to the main road the destination was on. We made our way up Bush Road to Houbolt, and crossed under I-80 before we reached the drive that would take us to the Joslin Junior College. The west side of the road looked fairly harmless, lots of trees and bushes, with the occasional pond thrown in for good measure. The other side of the street was what made me pause.

It was a huge subdivision, with hundreds, if not thousands of homes. If there was any lesson learned from the end of the world, it was subdivisions, especially in this country, either lived or died. There was no in between. Given this was Joslin, I knew that subdivision was dead, and nothing lived there. That gave us about three thousand potential zombies coming our way if things really turned against us. I hoped they had all drifted to the east when things had gotten bad, and had completely forgotten the way home.

Jake worked his way through a lot of broken driveway, and across a field that may have once been a parking lot, but it was hard to tell. In the distance, a huge building sat amid the trees and bushes, half of one side had completely collapsed, giving the building a lopsided look.

"Please tell me we don't have to try and dig through that mess," I said, unbuckling my seatbelt as we came to a stop.

"Hang on." Jake looked at the map he was holding, and then up at the building; then at the map, and then at the building. I was starting to get a bad feeling about this.

"Nope, we're good. It's supposed to be on the fifth floor of that building right in front of us." Jake put away the map and started putting his gear together. Julia pulled out her spear, and was about to belt on her knives and gun when she suddenly left the truck and walked through the tall grass of the parking lot. She went about twenty paces, and then suddenly stabbed down into the grass. Walking back, she wiped off her blade and smiled at us.

"Saw some grass move when it shouldn't have, and when I went over, I found a legless zombie working its way towards us. That would have been a nasty surprise when we came back to the truck," she said.

Nasty indeed. It was one thing to face a zombie head to head, no distractions. It was another to open a door and have one fall on you. That tended to darken your whole outlook for the day.

We loaded heavy after that, each of us taking our melee weapon and one of the secondary rifles we kept in the trucks. These were just .22 rifles, but they allowed us to carry a lot of ammo. Between the three of us, we could take on over fifteen hundred zombies if we had some good cover. Julia and Jake had Ruger 10/22s, while I had a Winchester 9422.

"All right, according to the information, there is a stairwell that takes up all the floors, and it should be right inside," Jake said.

"Let's go then," I said, feeling like this might be easy for a change.

"After you," Julia said brightly with a smile that didn't reach her eyes. I knew that look, and she was not about to be first.

Jake nodded, flicked off the safety of his rifle, and headed for the doors. The grass had taken over most of the parking lot, but it ended at the concrete steps towards the building. We looked around once we reached the top of the steps but did not see any more creepers in the tall grass.

The doors to the building were smashed in, and we carefully made our way around the broken glass. That was a good way to get infected, since the dead never worried about things like that and often cut themselves silly on broken glass. The virus lasted a long time in the open, and you could get infected by getting cut on zombie glass.

Inside, it was dark and musty. Mold grew all over the place and we quickly covered our faces with our bandanas. We tried to avoid stepping on any of it, because it was nasty when it was disturbed. Administrative offices were to our left if the fading signs were to be believed, but one look into the weird jungle that was growing there put our curiosity to rest. The high ceiling had a lot of spider webs all over the place, and as we got deeper into the building, I swore I could hear the spiders as they scuttled from place to place.

"Over here," Julia called us to the stairwell doors. Jake and I were surprised to find the doors not opening. We pushed, but they were stuck. I tried a final time, and managed to get the door to move an inch, which told me there was something on the other side.

Jake and I pushed again and this time the door slid open enough for Jake to get his head and a flashlight in to look around and see what was blocking it.

"Oh, man," Jake said, and managed to squeeze himself through the door. Julia and I waited on the outside and heard a lot of strange noises. Julia took the moment to try and sneak in a quick kiss, but our gear got in the way and we wound up giggling at each other.

Suddenly Jake opened the door and motioned us inside. We stepped in and saw a pile of corpses on the landing between this floor and the one below us.

"What the hell?" I asked.

"Just a pile of dead people blocking the door. Don't look like they were zombies, so I'm guessing they got trapped in here and chose to just die instead of being eaten or making a fight of it." Jake said.

That made no sense to me. If you were looking at death anyway, why not take out a few of your killers. That's what I always told myself I would do, anyway.

"Well, at least they weren't zombies when you stuck your head through the doorway," I said.

Julia tapped me on the arm. "Don't be silly. Jake wouldn't make a mistake like that." She winked and added. "He would never forget to lock the exit doors to keep the zombies from following him and wind up spending twelve hours in a women's bathroom."

I chuckled. "That's true. He would never, ever, think of not trying to arouse dormant zombies and get chased for three miles by the slowest group of ghouls we've ever seen. Not Jake."

Jake gave us both an evil stare before heading up the stairwell. It was dark as night in the enclosed space, and our flashlights weren't much help. The stairs were wide, and on a few steps, we could see old signs of trouble, like a splattering here or there, or some dark stains over the banister and doors.

CHAPTER 39

We reached the fifth floor without incident, and Jake opened the door with Julia and me at the ready with our rifles. Zombies that had been around for a while were decayed up to a point, and their bones weakened significantly. So much so that a little .22 was effectively able to kill a zombie given the weakness of their skulls. Fresher zombies needed a little heavier firepower.

The fifth floor was the library, and it had a huge wall of windows that allowed a lot of light in. That helped a great deal.

"Where's the thingy?" I asked, moving around a couple of tables to a map cabinet. Maps were extremely valuable, so I wasn't going to let this opportunity go to waste.

Jake looked around and spotted a glassed-in room with a lot of computers in it. "Over there, I'll be right back."

Julia wandered off to find some books of her own, while I dove into the maps. There were big road maps for all the states, plus a couple of county maps for Will, Cook, Dupage, Kane, and Kendall counties. These were a huge find, and I quickly rolled up the maps into a big tube. I tied off the two ends with a string and slung the whole bundle over my shoulder.

Julia came over a little while later, and she was holding about five books, all of them romance. When I gave her a lopsided grin, she just shrugged.

We waited for Jake, who took fifteen minutes to get back to us. He was holding what looked like it was another computer tower, only thicker.

"I think I got it," he panted. "I'm not one hundred percent sure, but it fit the description better than any of the others."

"Did you grab the power cord?" I asked. "I'm not coming back here for that."

Jake looked sheepish. He handed the server over to me and scooted back into the computer room. He came out with a small chord that he put into his backpack.

"That would have been embarrassing," he said.

"Especially since you'd have to come back alone," I said.

"What'd you find?" Jake asked, pointing to the rolls on my shoulder.

"Maps, including county maps," I said with a smile.

"Nice."

Julia had already tucked her books away, not giving Jake the pleasure of teasing her.

"Ready to go?" I asked.

"Right behind you," Jake said. He would have to be in back, since his hands were occupied with the collection. He couldn't just drop the thing and fight. That would defeat the purpose of this trip. We had a computer at home that we used from time to time, but this thing was something different. I found myself wondering what they were going to do with it, but it wasn't my worry.

We started down the stairs and immediately knew something was wrong. There was a lot of noise a couple of flights down and some banging, as if something was running into the walls. Julia shone her light down the stairwell and lit up about a dozen zombies. They must have been on levels we passed, and got into the stairs to chase after us.

"Back! Into the library!" Julia called out, causing a series of groans that echoed up and down the stairwell.

We dodged back into the library and closed the doors. I secured the handles with a big zip tie and hoped it would hold long enough to find another way down.

"Search the two sides, there has to be another way out of here," Jake said, heading off into the stacks. Julia and I split up, and I went over to the magazine section by the opposite walls.

About a minute later, there came a pounding on the door and a surging that stretched the zip tie. The zombies were groaning something fierce, and I could have sworn I heard answering groans, although it could have been an echo.

I found nothing, and I was running into Jake back at the center when Julia called out.

"Over here!"

We followed the sound of her voice and found her along the back wall next to a fire door. She was smiling as if she just got away with something, although neither Jake nor I felt like smiling back.

The door was tucked away behind a couple rows of books, and next to a small study booth. It would have taken us an hour to find this door and she walks right up to it. I had to ask.

"How did you find this door so fast?"

Julia didn't answer, she just pointed at the ceiling. Above us were exit signs that conveniently marked the way. Cute.

We stepped through the door just as we could hear the other door breaking open. The groans and moans got suddenly louder as the zombies, desperate for prey, began hunting through the aisles of books and materials. Just as the door was closing, I heard a sound that chilled me to the bone. It was the high-pitched wheezing of a child zombie.

Nothing was more dangerous than a little kid zombie. For whatever reason, they were fast, vicious, and smarter than your average zombie was. If you had one stalking you, you needed to find some open space really fast, and hope it wasn't right on your ass. No one knew why they were so different, but it didn't matter. They were and we had to be ready for them.

CHAPTER 40

We moved down the fire escape as quickly and as quietly as possible. If we were lucky, the little bastards wouldn't find the fire escape until it was too late. If we were very lucky, we would be out of here in a few minutes.

At the bottom of the stairs on the first floor, Julia halted by the door and looked out the little window. She shook her head, indicating she didn't see any zombies. Jake was sweating his ass off; apparently, the server was heavier than he had anticipated. I didn't offer to take it from him, and I knew he would be too proud to ask. It was amusing to see him make himself suffer like this.

Julia opened the door and I followed behind, with Jake bringing up the rear. We were at the end of a long balcony, with several small offices positioned on our right. On our left was open space, and the light coming in from the huge windows showed us an enormous hall, with dozens of large tables scattered about. I guessed that this was where the students to the college got something to eat when the mood hit them.

It was also the place where about fifty zombies were hanging out, and they groaned loudly as they made their way under the balcony to reach up in frustration at us. A large stairwell that I could see that went under the balcony on the other side and came out in the middle of the hallway in front of us. Several zombies were making their way to the stairs, and we didn't have much time.

"Let's go, let's go!" Julia urged Jake and me, although we had no plans for sticking around.

We ran across the balcony, and we were turning the corner to head out the front when Julia stopped dead. I ran into her trying to stop, and Jake ran into me. A corner of the server jabbed me in the back to add injury to insult.

I didn't ask why Julia had stopped. A big horde of zombies had come out of the dark and had been looking for us to return when we came at them from behind. Had we come down the stairs we had gone up, we would have walked right into the middle of them before we knew they were there.

"Follow me!" I said, turning around and running for the surprisingly well-lit bridge that linked this building with another across a small valley. We ran past the cafeteria stairwell that was becoming crowded with ghouls, and onto the bridge. The first section wasn't very bright, but that was because it looked to be a sitting room where students could watch the television that was mounted on the wall.

The next room was a big lounge area, with lots of small chairs and desks for work. The windows on this section of the bridge were clear, and it was as bright as day in that area. The next section had two little pits that went into the floor about five feet and more chairs and cushions were scattered about. There was also a large party of zombies headed our way from the other side.

"Watch yourself!" I yelled as I jumped into the pit, running across and leaping up the other side. I was hoping the other side of the bridge was unoccupied and I breathed an internal sigh of relief when I saw that it was.

I looked back to make sure Julia and Jake made it across, and Julia leapt up with a great deal of grace. Jake was doing well, but on his jump up, his foot caught the edge of the step and he went down. The server flew from his hands, past my startled head, and through the window. The glass seemed to fall for a long time as I watched the server drift away into space before landing at the bottom of the valley. Imagine my surprise when the valley floor splashed up as the server disappeared beneath the surface of the water down there.

I didn't say anything, I just looked through the big hole in disbelief. Jake got up and joined me at the hole.

"Where did it go? Can we go get it?" he asked.

"No," I said, ignoring the wave of zombies headed our way.

"Guys?" Julia asked.

"Why not? It's not that far. It probably landed on something soft." Jake argued.

"Guys?" Julia asked again.

"Soft like the pond it fell in?" I asked, pointing to the edge of the water that could be seen further out from the bridge.

Jake visibly deflated. "Well, *dang.*"

"*Guys!*" Julia yelled.

"What? Oh." We finally paid attention and realized the zombies were closing in behind, the side, and in front.

I whipped up my rifle and fired once, sending a hot round through the brain of a zombie, tumbling her to the floor. "I got the back, Jake, you take the front, and Julia, the side's yours. First one clear, we go that way."

We fired carefully, and some of our targets required more than one round, but we had enough ammo for a decent fight, as long as we took our time and made the shots count. .22s worked well on zombies, but you had to hit them straight it. Any angle made it risky to need a second shot, and if they were close enough, it was going to be tough.

After I had dropped fifteen zombies, I paused to reload. I had created enough of a barrier that the zombies were delayed tripping over their fallen comrades. I had a tubular magazine, so it wasn't as quick as using a semi-auto's magazine, but I could reload faster than they could reload their mags, so it evened out.

Suddenly, Julia shouted. "Clear!" We wasted no time in bolting across the lounge space one more time and heading right, moving towards the second building again. Behind us, dozens of zombies were in pursuit, and I stopped to shoot two of the others to try and trip up the rest to buy us some time.

Julia fired twice, killing a couple of ghouls that stumbled out of the doorway to the main area, and then we were clear.

"This way!" Jake said, running down a huge corridor. On the left were floor to ceiling windows, and this allowed us to see very well as we moved past tables, chairs, and a mess of used supplies. Apparently, someone in the past has used this place as a safe zone against zombies. With dozens of doors and huge windows, that was probably a mistake.

On our right were two floors of classrooms and several alcoves of lecture halls and experiment rooms. As we ran past room after room, I was struck with the size of the damn place.

You could effectively house a big community here and have room for everyone. That is, if you could keep the zombies from smashing your windows in.

"Come on!" Jake was running towards the far end of the hall, where a set of doors looked like they would lead us to the outside. We didn't need motivation, as zombies poured from the doorway to the bridge into the main hall. If there was one there was a hundred, and they all moved in groaning desperation for flesh.

I looked back and saw what I feared most. Several little zombies were outrunning their peers and were moving up on us fast. I stopped suddenly, firing once, and managed to put one of them down.

Jake looked back to see what I was doing and cursed. "Damn. Just keep on running Aaron, we'll get them outside!"

I spun around and caught up to Jake and Julia, and we put on an additional burst of speed to get away from the little ones. At the doors, we nearly broke them in an attempt to get through, and I tied the interior doors with a zip tie. The exterior doors got the same treatment, and we moved away from the building and into the parking lot.

CHAPTER 41

Rather, what was left of it. Nature had been staking claims on this property for years, and in recent times had made pretty good progress. But there were wide spaces and little cover, so it would be a good place to make a stand.

Behind us, the glass on the door shattered, and four little zombies shoved their way through the broken shards, slicing themselves silly on the glass. They were going to look worse than they already did, if that was possible.

Jake led us south through the parking lot and towards the small valley that was home to the big pond that swallowed our server. He went right up to the edge, and then turned around. Julia and I turned as well, but Jake shook his head.

"Nope. You two get down on the hill, further south and stay out of sight. We need an advantage here and with four to three odds, one of us will get killed if we stand together," he said.

"What are you going to do?" I asked, pulling out my sword. "You can't face them alone."

"You'll see. Just be ready to get up here in a hurry," Jake said.

I shook my head, but I did as he wanted. Julia and I moved about fifteen feet away and then hunkered down just over the edge of the ditch. It was a steep ditch, so it wasn't easy to stay in place, let alone get out in a hurry, but we'd have it to do.

Jake stood on the edge of the ditch, watching the little zombies streak towards him. I couldn't see where they were, but I gauged how close they were by how tightly Jake was clenching his jaw. I could hear them moving through the grass, and their weird wheezing was getting louder and louder.

Suddenly, Jake jumped back, ducked down, and four little zombies flew over him and into the ditch. We all jumped up and out of the grass and stood waiting for the zombies to return. They fell nearly to the water's edge, then scrambled as best they could for the grass and started up the hill towards us. In their haste, they slipped and fell a lot, spreading them out and making it easier for us to deal with them.

Julia killed the first one as it poked its nasty head over the edge of the grass. About ten feet to the left, another one reached the top, only to be cracked on the skull by Jake's mace. Julia killed the next one, and Jake finished the last.

"No work for you, sorry," Julia said sweetly.

"No cleaning of my sword, sorry," I replied, just as sweetly. Julia frowned at that.

Jake wiped his mace off in the grass, and pointed at the door we had exited. Several zombies were getting out, and heading our way. "We need to settle that first; otherwise, the communities to the south and west are really going to be mad."

"Got it," I said. We ran back towards the building, and used our rifles to shoot down the zombies that had already gotten outside. When that was finished, we set up a system where Julia would shoot the zombies as they came out the doors, Jake would reload the rifles, and I would drag the zombie away so they wouldn't pile up and cause a blockage. It was slow, tedious work, but since we lost the server, we really had nothing else to do for the day.

When the last zombie had crawled its way out, only to be shot dead for its efforts, we all stretched and took the long walk back to the truck. We spread out, scanning the grass for any additional threats. When none was jumping out at us, we finally relaxed and began putting away our weapons. Jake and Julia cleaned their gear while I stowed away the rifles and ammo.

We pulled away from the college. I couldn't help wondering what it had been like when there weren't any zombies around, and people came here to learn something.

We weren't too bummed out about the server. While the money would have been nice, we really didn't need it, and it wasn't the first collection we had lost. There was a time in Chicago when Jake and I were trying to retrieve a silverware collection that wound up scattered over half of Michigan Avenue when I hadn't realized the box had opened. Such was the way of things.

We drove north towards the capital, and we were all lost in our thoughts as the prospect of starting something new was now staring us in the face. We had an obligation to fulfill, as the very fragile country we were in was in need of help, and there was no one else to take on the job. The old guard, the ones who had fought the wars and survived the zombies, was getting older. While still able to fight, they would be outnumbered by the younger generation who hadn't fought, and who hadn't trained. These days, kids were taught avoidance, not confrontation with the undead.

This situation was to the advantage of those who wanted to use the zombies as a weapon for their own purposes.

As far as I could tell, we were the only ones standing in the way.

CHAPTER 42

"What do you mean you had it but it's gone?" The man was clearly irritated at the news Jake had to report.

"If I tell you several times, it isn't going to change the outcome, so you may as well pay closer attention to the last time I'm going to inform you of the whereabouts of the server," Jake said deliberately. "There was a situation that occurred and the server is now at the bottom of a pond. You're welcome to go for it yourself or hire another collector, but we're done."

"Do you know what that server meant?" The man, a short, squatty person with pig-eyes and a bad goatee, could barely contain his irritation. However, his ire was tempered by the fact that I was scowling fiercely at the way he was speaking to my brother, and I was easily head and shoulders taller than he was.

Jake shrugged. "Don't know, don't care. As I said, we're all done. If it matters, it looked like there was a second server there, so you can send someone else out for it. Here's your down payment, minus ten gold pieces for our trouble." Jake tossed the man the tube of coins he had originally been paid.

"What? You fail, yet you keep twenty percent? What the hell? I guess I can believe what I hear about you collectors." The man sneered in Jake's face and I was sure Jake was going to pound him for it, but Jake remained calm.

"Consider it payment for information regarding the second server. *I* will, and I'll ignore your insult and let you keep your face the way it is." Jake's eyes were dangerously narrow, and the next thing the man said would determine whether he kept all of his body parts in one convenient place.

The man considered that and survival conquered pride. "Well, it's still steep, but perhaps you can recommend someone else?"

Jake snorted. "Not likely. But you can keep the rest of that coin yourself, and tell your investors we kept it as a non-refundable down payment. I don't really care." With that, Jake turned away from the man who was suddenly very interested in the coins.

I turned away in disgust and followed Jake, with Julia walking alongside. We headed down towards the information center, where we typically got our requests for collections. It wasn't much, just a store that had been converted to bunch of bulletin boards. We rented a small space, and people tacked notes and information for us and we took those we were interested in.

"Hey, Bill!" Jake called. Bill was the owner of the information center, and charged a copper a month for a square foot of space, more for larger spaces. The church owned the largest, and it was full of notices of people looking for relatives or information about relatives. The hardest ones to look at were notices about children. There was usually no hope whatsoever, but people had to try something, if they weren't willing to go out themselves.

Another space that was available for no charge was a missing person's board, and there were a lot of notices about people who had gone missing. I looked over a few and noticed overwhelmingly they were girls between the ages of sixteen and twenty. A few older women were posted, but not many. I idly wondered where they all could have gone.

"Hey, Jake! How's business?" Bill was an older gentleman, one of the founders of the new capitol. He had come along with our fathers, and he was a solid, dependable man. Truth be known, he was a good fighter, too, and had held his own against the last major zombie outbreak.

"Finished. We're not collecting anymore." Jake related what we had been through and what we suspected. He also spoke briefly, about what we planned on doing, and Bill had only one thing to say.

"About time. You need help. Just ask. There's a lot of us old timers who have seen what we built start to slide back and didn't know what to do about it. You need anything, just let me know." Bill was dead serious, and if I didn't know better, I'd say he was half tempted to join us.

"Thanks, but I think the fewer that are aware, the better. We'll be all right. It's what we're supposed to do," Jake said.

"Yes, you are," Bill replied, and he nodded to each of us in turn. Julia took my hand and Bill noticed. He smiled and said to Julia. "Your dad would be very happy for you."

Julia smiled. "I hope to tell him myself."

Bill nodded. "He'll be back." Bill looked at Jake and me. "They both will."

We shook hands and headed out into the street. The sun was just past noon, so we decided to treat ourselves to a meal we didn't have to make ourselves. We stopped at the Constitution Café, so named for the document that was housed in the legislative building. That was a story in itself and one I don't feel like relating.

We ate well, ignoring the curious glances our outfits aroused in the locals, and stepping out into the street we found ourselves staring at four men we had seen before. Carson Casey was standing in front of three other men, and he was grinning broadly. He spoke to Jake.

"Well, well. Thought I saw you in town. Good thing, too. I was missing that sweet piece of ass you got behind you."

Jake didn't say anything and he held up a hand to keep me from stepping off the sidewalk.

"Carson Casey. Well, I wondered where all the shit in town wound up," Jake said, stepping forward.

Carson turned red and pulled a long knife from his belt. "I'll cut that smart-ass tongue out of your mouth, boy!"

"You've got it to do." Jake moved suddenly and Casey howled. A line thing line appeared on his forearm and started to bleed all over the place.

Casey grabbed his wound and stared at Jake, who stood casually waiting for Carson to move again. Carson snarled and lunged forward, stabbing his blade towards Jake's eyes. Jake waited for the last possible second, and then knocked the blade away, stepping away from the lunge and stabbing Carson in the shoulder.

Carson howled and his arm hung down at his side, his knife useless. One of the men stepped forward with his hands raised and I took that moment to step up. I shot a punch straightforward, right past his hands and into his face. I felt his nose crunch beneath my fist and his head snapped back. His legs gave way and he crumpled to the ground to lie there and bleed.

Carson grabbed his knife with his other hand, and tried a cut at Jake. Jake easily dodged and rammed his knife forward, burying the blade in Casey's throat. Carson fell to the ground, clutching at the hilt that protruded from his neck. He lay on his back, his feet drumming uselessly on the ground while he slowly drowned in his own blood. The drumming weakened, and then stopped altogether.

The remaining two men had seen enough, and they turned to run. One made it away, but the other fell to the ground with a thrown tomahawk in his leg. He screamed as I pulled it out and I punched him in the face to quiet him. When he was done, I placed the point of the spike end on his cheek and edged it towards his eye.

"Who's your boss?" I asked.

"He was," the answer came.

'Bullshit. He was just muscle. Who gave him orders?' I demanded.

"He got his orders from someone else, don't know who."

"Where do the orders come from?" Jake asked.

The man wet his lips, but gasped when I broke the skin just under his eye. "Zoomertown. He goes to Zoomertown."

"New rules. You and your kind are not allowed here anymore. We're coming to clean you out," I said, and the man nodded carefully, never taking his eye off my spike.

I let the man up, and just as he scuttled out of sight, Lane Tucker showed up with four of his deputies. Lane took in the scene, and dispatched one of his deputies to talk to the customers of the Café to see if their story will match ours.

"Well. I'd say you stepped in it this time. Can't say, as I'll miss Casey, though. Never seen this guy before." Tucker looked over the unconscious man and motioned to one of his men to put handcuffs on the man. The deputy returned from the café and spoke quietly to Tucker.

Lane addressed us. "Well, you're free to go. Watch your back, though. You've beaten these guys once, and they'll remember you."

"I hope they do, Tucker," I said.

Lane Tucker looked at me, and then nodded slowly. "It might be a good idea to see me before you go out after anyone."

"Why?" Julia asked.

"As you are, you're vigilantes, and we don't tolerate that kind of behavior. But if, suppose, someone were to make deputies out of you, with special jurisdiction outside of the capitol, well, that might avoid some difficult questions," Tucker said.

Whatever I was going to say had to wait. A young boy ran up holding a piece of paper. He goggled a bit at the two prone men, but remembered his mission quickly enough. "Are you Jake?" the boy asked me.

"Nope. That mean looking cuss is Jake," I said, pointing at my brother.

"Mr. Jake, Mr. Bill sent this note." The boy handed Jake the note, and took the copper Jake gave him.

Jake read the note, and then handed it to me. He spoke to Lane. "We have to move. There's been a suspicious outbreak by St Charles." Jake looked at Julia and me. "Let's get moving."

We followed Jake and Julia whispered to me. "Does this mean what I think it does?"

I gave her a hand to squeeze. "Yep. It begins now."

THE END

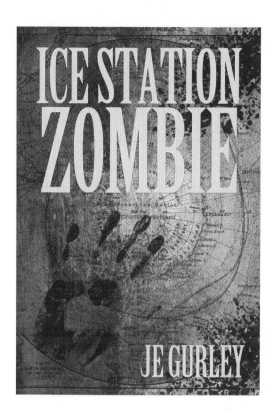

ICE STATION ZOMBIE
JE GURLEY

For most of the long, cold winter, Antarctica is a frozen wasteland. Now, the ice is melting and the zombies are thawing. Arctic explorers Val Marino and Elliot Anson race against time and death to reach Australia, but the Demise has preceded them and zombies stalk the streets of Adelaide and Coober Pedy.

www.severedpress.com

The Coalition

When the dead rose to destroy the living, Ron Cutter learned to survive. While so many others died, he thrived. His life is a constant battle against the living dead. As he casts his own bullets and packs his shotgun shells, his humanity slowly melts away.

Then he encounters a lost boy and a woman searching for a place of refuge. Can they help him recover the emotions he set aside to live? And if he does recover them, will those feelings be an asset in his struggles, or a danger to him?

THE STATE OF EXTINCTION: the first installment in the **COALITON OF THE LIVING** trilogy of Mankind's battle against the plague of the Living Dead. As recounted by author **Robert Mathis Kurtz.**

www.severedpress.com

RANCID

Nothing ever happens in the middle of nowhere or in Virginia for that matter. This is why Noel and her friends found themselves on cloud nine when one of their favorite hardcore bands happened to be playing a show in their small hometown. Between the meteor shower and the short trip to the cemetery outside of town after the show, this crazy group of friends instantly plummet from those clouds into a frenzied nightmare of putrefied horror.

Is this sudden nightmare related to the showering meteors or does this small town hold even darker secrets than the rotting corpses that are surfacing?

"Zombies in small town America, a corporate conspiracy, fast paced action and a satisfying body count- what's not to like? Just don't get too attached to any character; they may die or turn zombie soon enough!" - Mainak Dhar, bestselling author of Alice in Deadland and Zombiestan

www.severedpress.com

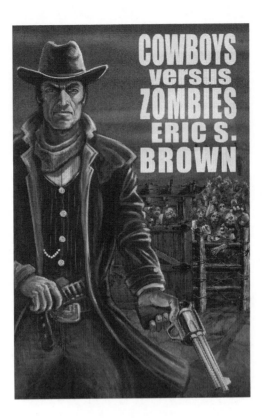

COWBOYS VS ZOMBIES

Dilouie is a killer. He's always made his way in life by the speed of his gun hand and the coldness of his remorseless heart. Life never meant much to him until the world fell apart and they awoke. Overnight, the dead stopped being dead. Hungry corpses rose from blood splattered streets and graves. Their numbers were unimaginable and their need for the flesh of the living insatiable.

The United States is no more. Washed away in a tide of gnashing teeth and rotting, clawing hands. Dilouie no longer kills for money and pleasure but to simply keep breathing and to see the sunrise of the next dawn. . . And he is beginning to wonder if even men like him can survive in a world that now belongs to the dead?

TIMOTHY
MARK TUFO

Timothy was not a good man in life and being
undead did little to improve his disposition.
Find out what a man trapped in his own mind
will do to survive when he wakes up to find
himself a zombie controlled by a self-aware
virus.

www.severedpress.com

Printed in Great Britain
by Amazon.co.uk, Ltd.,
Marston Gate.